A TALE OF TWO CITIES

BY

CHARLES DICKENS

READ BY

JOHN CARSON

Text has been abridged for recording by Sam Curtis
Produced by Graham Goodwin
Read-Along © 1986 ALS Audio Language Studies Inc.

"USA Patent No. 4141446, USA and Canadian Patent Applications Pending"
**MANUFACTURED AND PRINTED IN CANADA BY
ALS AUDIO LANGUAGE STUDIES INC.,
25 MALLARD ROAD
DON MILLS, ONTARIO, CANADA M3B 1S4**

A Tale of Two Cities is Charles Dickens' famous tale set against the background of the French Revolution. Doctor Manette, his devoted daughter Lucie and the young French aristocrat Charles Darnay are memorable characters etched by the skillful pen of Dickens, but above all the others rises the reckless Sydney Carton, whose selfless love makes him one of literature's great heroes.

INDEX

It was the best of times. It was the worst of times. It was the age of wisdom. It was the age of foolishness. It was the epoch of belief. It was the epoch of incredulity. It was the season of Light. It was the season of Darkness.

There was a king with a large jaw and a queen with a plain face on the throne of England. There was a king with a large jaw and a queen with a fair face on the throne of France.

It was the year of Our Lord one thousand seven hundred and seventy-five.

France, less favored on the whole as to matters spiritual than her sister of the shield and trident, rolled with exceeding smoothness downhill, making paper money and spending it. It is likely enough that in the rough outhouses of some tillers of the heavy lands adjacent to Paris, there were, sheltered from the weather that very day, rude carts, bespattered with rustic mire, snuffed about by pigs and roosted in by poultry, which the Farmer, Death, had already set apart to be his tumbrels of the Revolution.

In England, there was scarcely an amount of order and protection to justify much national boasting. Daring burglaries by armed men and highway robberies took place in the capital itself every night. The Lord Mayor of London was made to stand and deliver on Turnham Green by one highwayman who despoiled the illustrious creature in sight of all his retinue; prisoners in London jails fought battles with their turnkeys.

These things, and a thousand like them, came to pass in and close upon the dear old year one thousand seven hundred and seventy-five. Thus did the year conduct the great and myriads of small creatures--the creatures of this chronicle among the rest--along the roads that lay before them.

It was the Dover road that lay, on a Friday night late in November, before the first of the persons with whom this history has business. The Dover road lay--as to him--beyond the Dover mail, as it lumbered up

Shooter's Hill. He walked uphill in the mire by the side of the mail, as the rest of the passengers did, not because they had the least relish for walking exercise, under the circumstances, but because the hill, and the harness, and the mud, and the mail, were all so heavy that the horses had three times already come to a stop, besides once drawing the coach across the road, with the mutinous intent of taking it back to Blackheath.

Two other passengers, besides the one, were plodding up the hill by the side of the mail. All three were wrapped to the cheek-bones and over the ears and wore jack-boots. Not one of the three could have said, from anything he saw, what either of the other two was like. And each was hidden under almost as many wrappers from the eyes of the mind as from the eyes of the body of his two companions. In those days, travelers were very shy of being confidential on a short notice, for anybody on the road might be a robber or in league with robbers.

The last burst carried the mail to the summit of the hill. The horses stopped to breath again. The guard got down to skid the wheel for the descent and open the coach-door to let the passengers in.

"Pst! Joe!" cried the coachman in a warning voice, looking down from his box.

"What do you say, Tom?"

They both listened.

"I say a horse at a canter coming up, Joe."

"I say a horse at a gallop, Tom," returned the guard, leaving his hold on the door and mounting nimbly to his place. "Gentlemen! In the king's name, all of you!"

With this hurried adjuration, he cocked his blunderbuss and stood on the offensive.

The sound of a horse at a gallop came fast and furiously up the hill.

"So-ho!" the guard sang out, as loud as he could roar. "Yo there! Stand! I shall fire!"

The pace was suddenly checked, and, with much splashing and floundering, a man's voice called from the mist, "Is that the Dover mail?"

"Why do you want to know?" the guard retorted.

"I want a passenger, if it is."

"What passenger?"

"Mr. Jarvis Lorry."

Our booked passenger showed in a moment that it was his name. The guard, the coachman, and the two other passengers eyed him distrustfully.

"What is the matter?" asked the passenger. Then, with mildly quavering speech, "Wh-wh-who wants me? Is it Jerry?"

"Yes, Mr. Lorry."

"What is the matter?"

"A dispatch sent to you from over yonder. T. and Co."

"I know this messenger, guard," said Mr. Lorry, getting down into the road--assisted from behind more swiftly than politely by the two other passengers, who immediately scrambled into the coach, shut the door, and pulled up the window. "He may come close. There's nothing wrong."

The figures of a horse and rider came slowly through the eddying mist and came to the side of the mail where the passenger stood. The rider stopped, and, casting up his eyes at the guard, handed the passenger a small folded paper. The rider's horse was blown, and both horse and rider were covered with mud, from the hoofs of the horse to the hat of the man.

"Guard!" said the passenger, in a tone of quiet business confidence.

The watchful guard, with his right hand at the stock of his raised blunderbuss, his left at the barrel, and his eye on the horseman, answered curtly, "Sir."

"There is nothing to apprehend. I belong to Tellson's Bank. You must know Tellson's Bank in London. I am going to Paris on business. I may read this?"

"So be as you're quick, sir."

He opened it in the light of the coach-lamp on that side, and read, first to himself and then aloud, "'Wait at Dover for Mam'selle.' It's not long, you see, guard. Jerry, say that my answer is, 'Recalled to life.'"

Jerry started in his saddle. "That's a blazing strange answer, too," said he, at his hoarsest.

"Take that message back, and they will know that I received this as well as if I wrote. Make the best of your way. Good night."

With those words, the passenger opened the coach-door and got in.

The coach lumbered on again with heavier wreaths of mist closing round it as it began the descent.

When the mail had got successfully to Dover, in the course of the forenoon, the head drawer at the Royal George Hotel opened the coach-door as his custom was.

The mildewy inside of the coach, with its damp and dirty straw, its disagreeable smell, and its obscurity, was rather like a larger dog-kennel. Mr. Lorry, the passenger, shaking himself out of it in chains of straw, a tangle of shaggy wrapper, flapping hat and muddy legs, was rather like a larger sort of dog.

"There will be a packet to Calais tomorrow, drawer?"

"Yes, sir, if the weather holds and the wind sets

tolerable fair. The tide will serve pretty nicely at about two in the afternoon, sir. Bed, sir?"

"I shall not go to bed till night. But I want a bedroom, and a barber."

"And then breakfast, sir? Yes, sir. That way, sir, if you please."

The coffee-room had no other occupant that forenoon than the passenger. His breakfast-table was drawn before the fire, and as he sat with its light shining on him, waiting for the meal, he sat so still that he might have been sitting for his portrait.

Soon, completing his resemblance to a man who was sitting for his portrait, Mr. Lorry dropped off to sleep. The arrival of his breakfast roused him, and he said to the drawer as he moved his chair to it:

"I wish accommodation prepared for a young lady who may come here at any time to-day. She may ask for Mr. Jarvis Lorry, or she may only ask for a gentleman from Tellson's Bank. Please to let me know."

"Yes, sir. Tellson's Bank in London, sir?"

"Yes."

"Yes, sir. We have oftentimes the honor to entertain your gentlemen in their traveling backwards and forwards betwixt London and Paris, sir. A vast deal of traveling, sir, in Tellson and Company's house."

"Yes. We are quite a French House as well as an English one."

"Yes, sir. Not much in the habit of such traveling yourself, I think, sir?"

"Not of late years. It is fifteen years since we-- since I--last came from France."

When Mr. Lorry had finished his breakfast, he went out for a stroll on the beach. The little narrow, crooked town of Dover hid itself away from the beach, and ran its head into the tall cliffs like a marine ostrich. The beach was a desert of heaps of sea and stones tumbling wildly about, and the sea did what it liked, and what it liked was destruction. It thundered at the town and thundered at the cliffs and brought the coast down, madly.

As the day declined into the afternoon, and the air, which had been at intervals clear enough to allow the French coast to be seen, became again charged with mist and vapor, Mr. Lorry's thoughts seemed to cloud too. When it was dark, as he sat before the coffee-room fire, his mind was busily digging, digging, digging, in the live red coals.

In a very few minutes the waiter came in to announce that Miss Manette had arrived from London and would be happy to see the gentleman from Tellson's.

"So soon?"

Miss Manette had taken some refreshment on the road, and required none then, and was extremely anxious to see the gentleman from Tellson's immediately, if it suited his pleasure and convenience.

The gentleman from Tellson's had nothing left for it but to empty his glass with an air of stolid desperation, settle his odd little flaxen wig at the ears, and follow the waiter to Miss Manette's apartment. It was a large, dark room, furnished in a funereal manner with black horse-hair, and loaded with heavy dark tables. These had been oiled and oiled, until the two tall candles on the table in the middle of the room were gloomily reflected on every leaf, as if they were buried, in deep graves of black mahogany, and no light to speak of could be expected from them until they were dug out.

The obscurity was so difficult to penetrate that Mr. Lorry, picking his way over the well-worn Turkey carpet, supposed Miss Manette to be, for the moment, in some adjacent room, until, having got past the two tall candles, he saw, standing to receive him, by the table between them and the fire, a young lady of not more than seventeen, in a riding cloak and still holding her straw traveling hat by its ribbon in her hand.

"Pray take a seat, sir," in a very clear and pleasant young voice, a little foreign in its accent, but a very little indeed.

"I kiss your hand, miss," said Mr. Lorry, with the manners of an earlier date, as he made his formal bow again and took his seat.

"I received a letter from the Bank yesterday, informing me that some intelligence--or discovery--"

"The word is not material, miss. Either word will do."

"--respecting the small property of my poor father, whom I never saw--so long dead--rendered it necessary that I should go to Paris, there to communicate with a gentleman of the Bank, so good as to be dispatched to Paris for the purpose."

"Myself."

"Are you quite a stranger to me, sir?"

"Am I not?" Mr. Lorry opened his hands, and extended them outwards with an argumentative smile. "Miss Manette, I am a man of business. I have a business charge to acquit myself of. In your reception of it, don't heed me anymore than if I was a speaking machine. Truly, I am not much more. I will, with your leave, relate to you, miss, the story of one of our customers."

"Story!"

He seemed wilfully to mistake the word she had repeated, when he added in a hurry, "Yes, customers. In the banking business we usually call our connection our customers. He was a French gentleman, a scientific gentleman, a man of great acquirements--a doctor."

"Not of Beauvais?"

"Why, yes, of Beauvais. Like Monsieur Manette, your father, the gentleman was of repute in Paris. I had the honor of knowing him there. Our relations were business relations, but confidential. I was at that time in our French House, and had been--oh! twenty years."

"At that time--I may ask, at what time, sir?"

"I speak, miss, of twenty years ago. He married an English lady, and I was one of the trustees. His affairs, like the affairs of many other French gentlemen and French families, were entirely in Tellson's hands. In a similar way I am, or I have been, trustee of one kind or other for scores of our customers. These are mere business relations, miss. There is no friendship in them, no particular interest, nothing like sentiment. I have passed from one to another, in the course of my business life, just as I pass from one of our customers to another in the course of my business day. In short, I have no feelings. I am a mere machine. To go on--"

"But this is my father's story, sir. And I begin to think that when I was left an orphan, through my mother's surviving my father only two years, it was you who brought me to England. I am almost sure it was you."

"Miss Manette, it was I. So far, Miss, as you have remarked, this is the story of your regretted father. Now comes the difference. If your father had not died when he did--don't be frightened! How you do start!"

She did, indeed, start. And she caught his wrist with both her hands.

"As I was saying: if Monsieur Manette had not died; if he had suddenly and silently disappeared; if he had been spirited away; if it had not been difficult to guess to what dreadful place, though no art could trace him; if he had an enemy in some compatriot who could exercise a privilege that I in my own time have known the boldest people afraid to speak of in a whisper, across the water there; if his wife had implored the king, the queen, the court, the clergy, for any tidings of him, and all quite in vain, then the history of your father would have been the history of this unfortunate gentleman, the Doctor of Beauvais.

"I entreat you to tell me more, sir."

"I will. I am going to. Now, if this doctor's wife, though a lady of great courage and spirit, had suffered so intensely from this cause before her little child was born--"

"The little child was a daughter, sir?"

"A daughter. Miss, if the poor lady had suffered so intensely before her little child was born, that she came to the determination of sparing the poor child the inheritance of any part of the agony she had known the pains of, by rearing her in the belief that her father was dead--No! No, no, no, don't kneel! In Heaven's name why should you kneel to me?"

"For the truth. Oh, dear, good, compassionate sir, for the truth!"

"Courage! Business! You have business before you, useful business. Miss Manette, your mother took this course with you. And when she died--I believe broken-hearted--having never slackened her unavailing search for your father, she left you, at two years old, to grow to be blooming, beautiful, and happy, without the dark cloud upon you of living in uncertainty whether your father soon wore his heart out in prison or wasted there through many lingering years.

"You know that your parents had no great possession, and that what they had was secured to your mother and to you. There has been no new discovery, of money, or of any other property. But--but he has been--been found. He is alive. Greatly changed, it is too probable; almost a wreck, it is possible; though we will hope for the best. Still, alive! Your father has been taken to the house of an old servant in Paris, and we are going there: I, to identify him if I can; you, to restore him to life, love, duty, rest, and comfort."

A shiver ran through her frame, and from it, through his. She said, in a low, distinct, awe-stricken voice, as if she were saying it in a dream:

"I am going to see his ghost! It will be his ghost, not him!"

Perfectly still and silent and not even fallen back in her chair, she sat under his hand, utterly insensible, with her eyes open and fixed upon him, and with that last expression looking as if it were carved or branded into her forehead. So close was her hold upon his arm that he feared to detach himself, lest he should hurt her. Therefore he called out loudly for assistance without moving.

A wild-looking woman came running into the room in advance of the inn servants and soon settled the question of his detachment from the poor young lady by laying a brawny hand upon his chest and sending him flying back against the nearest wall.

She softly laid the patient on a sofa and tended her with great skill and tenderness, calling her "my precious" and "my bird" and spreading her golden hair aside over her shoulders with great pride and care.

"I hope she will do well, now," said Mr. Lorry.

"No thanks to you, if she does. My darling pretty!"

"I hope," said Mr. Lorry, after another pause of feeble sympathy and humility, "that you accompany Miss Manette to France?"

"A likely thing, too!" replied the strong woman. "If it was ever intended that I should go across salt water, do you suppose Providence would have cast my lot in an island?"

This being a question hard to answer, Mr. Jarvis Lorry withdrew to consider it.

A large cask of wine had been dropped and broken in the street. The accident had happened in getting it out of a cart; the cask had tumbled out with a run, the hoops had burst, and it lay on the stones just outside the door of the wine-shop, shattered like a walnut shell.

All the people within reach had suspended their business or their idleness to run to the spot and drink the wine.

The wine was red wine and had stained the ground of the narrow street in the suburb of Saint Antoine in Paris, where it was spilled. It had stained many hands, too, and many faces and many naked feet and many wooden shoes.

The wine shop was a corner shop, better than most others in its appearance and degree, and the master of the wine shop had stood outside it in a yellow waistcoat and green breeches, looking on at the struggle for the lost wine.

"It was not my affair," said he, with a final shrug of the shoulders. "The people from the market did it. Let them bring another."

The wine-shop keeper was a bull-necked, martial-looking man of thirty, and he should have been of a hot temperament, for, although it was a bitter day, he wore no coat, but carried one slung over his shoulder. Good-humored looking on the whole, but implacable-looking, too.

Madame Defarge, his wife, sat in the shop behind the counter as he came in. Madame Defarge was a stout woman, of about his own age, with a watchful eye that seldom seemed to look at anything, a large hand heavily ringed, a steady face, strong features, and great composure of manner. Madame Defarge said nothing when her lord came in, but coughed--just one grain of cough. This, in combination with the lifting of her darkly defined eyebrows, suggested to her husband that he would do well to look around the shop among the customers, for any new customer who had dropped in while he stepped over the way.

The wine-shop keeper accordingly rolled his eyes about until they rested upon an elderly gentleman and a young lady who were seated in a corner. Other company were there: two playing cards, two playing dominoes, three standing by the counter lengthening out a short supply of wine. As he passed behind the counter, he took notice that the elderly gentleman said, in a look, to the young lady, "This is our man."

"What the devil do you do in that galley there?" said Monsieur Defarge to himself. "I don't know you."

But, he feigned not to notice the two strangers and fell into discourse with the triumvirate of customers who were drinking at the counter.

Finally, the three paid for their wine and left the place. The eyes of Monsieur Defarge were studying his wife at her knitting when the elderly gentleman advanced from his corner and begged the favor of a word.

"Willingly, sir," said Monsieur Defarge and quietly stepped with him to the door.

Their conference was very short, but very decided. Almost at the first word, Monsieur Defarge started and became deeply attentive. It had not lasted a minute when he nodded and went out. The gentleman then beckoned to the young lady, and they, too, went out.

Madame Defarge knitted with nimble fingers and steady eyebrows and saw nothing.

Mr. Jarvis Lorry and Miss Manette, emerging from the wine-shop, joined Monsieur Defarge in the doorway to which he had directed his other company just before. It opened from a stinking little black courtyard and was the general public entrance to a great pile of houses, inhabited by a great number of people. In the gloomy, tile-paved entry was a gloomy, tile-paved staircase.

"It is very high. It is a little difficult. Better to begin slowly," said Monsieur Defarge in a stern voice, to Mr. Lorry as they began ascending the stairs.

"Is he alone?" the latter whispered.

"Alone! God help him, who should be with him?" said the other in the same low voice.

At last, the top of the staircase was gained. There was yet an upper staircase of a steeper inclination and of contracted dimensions to be ascended before the garret story was reached.

They went up slowly and softly and were soon at the

top. With an admonitory gesture to keep them back, the keeper of the wine-shop stopped and looked in through a crevice in the wall.

The door slowly opened inward under his hand, and he looked into the room and said something. A faint voice answered something. Little more than a single syllabie could have been spoken on either side. He looked back over his shoulder and beckoned them to enter.

The garret, built to be a depository for firewood and the like, was dim and dark. It was difficult, on first coming in, to see anything. And long habit alone could have slowly formed in any one, the ability to do any work requiring nicety in such obscurity. Yet, work of that kind was being done in the garret. For, with his back towards the door and his face towards the window where the keeper of the wine-shop stood looking at him, a white-haired main sat on a low bench, stooping forward and very busy, making shoes.

"Good-day!" said Monsieur Defarge, looking down at the white head that bent low over the shoemaking.

It was raised for a moment, and a very faint voice responded to the salutation as if it were at a distance:

"Good-day!"

"You are still hard at work, I see?"

After a long silence, the head was lifted for another moment, and the voice replied, "Yes, I am working." This time a pair of haggard eyes had looked at the questioner before the face had dropped again.

The faintness of the voice was pitiable and dreadful.

"Are you going to finish that pair of shoes today?" said Defarge, motioning to Mr. Lorry to come forward.

"What did you say?"

"Do you mean to finish that pair of shoes today?"

"I can't say that I mean to. I suppose so. I don't know."

But the question reminded him of his work and he bent over it again.

Mr. Lorry came silently forward, leaving the daughter by the door.

"You have a visitor, you see," said Monsieur Defarge.

"What did you say?"

"Here is a visitor."

The shoemaker looked up as before, but without removing a hand from his work.

"Come," said Defarge. "Here is monsieur, who knows a well-made shoe when he sees one. Show him that shoe you are working at. Take it, monsieur."

Mr. Lorry took it in his hand.

"Tell monsieur what kind of shoe it is and the maker's name."

"Did you ask me for my name?"

"Assuredly I did."

"One Hundred and Five, North Tower."

"Is that all?"

"One Hundred and Five, North Tower."

With a weary sound, that was not a sigh, nor a groan, he began to work again, until the silence was again broken.

"You are not a shoemaker by trade?" said Mr. Lorry, looking steadfastly at him.

"I am not a shoemaker by trade? No, I was not a shoemaker by trade. I learnt it here. I taught myself. I asked leave to teach myself and I got it, with much difficulty, after a long time, and I have made shoes ever since."

"Monsieur Manette"--Mr. Lorry laid his hand upon Defarge's arm--"do you remember nothing of this man? Look at him. Look at me. Is there no old banker, no old business, no old servant, no old time, rising in your mind, Monsieur Manette?"

As the captive of many years sat looking fixedly, by turns, at Mr. Lorry and at Defarge, some long-obliterated marks of an actively intent intelligence, in the middle of the forehead, gradually forced themselves through the black mist that had fallen on him. They were overclouded again, they were fainter, they were gone. But they had been there.

Now Lucie moved from the wall of the garret, where

she had been watching, very near to the bench on which he sat.

He stared at her with a fearful look, and after a while his lips began to form some words, though no sound proceeded from them. By degrees, in the pauses of his quick and labored breathing, he was heard to say:

"What, what is this?"

With the tears streaming down her face, she put her two hands to her lips, and kissed them to him, then clasped them to her breast, as if she laid his ruined head there.

"You are not the jailer's daughter?"

She sighed, "No."

"Who are you?"

Not yet trusting the tones of her voice, she sat down on the bench beside him. He recoiled, but she laid her hand upon his arm. A strange thrill struck him when she did so, and visibly passed over his frame. He laid the knife down softly as he sat staring at her.

Her golden hair, which she wore in long curls had

been hurriedly pushed aside and fell down over her neck. Advancing his hand, by little and little, he took it up and looked at it. In the midst of the action he went astray, and with another deep sigh fell to work at his shoemaking.

But not for long. Releasing his arm, she laid her hand upon his shoulder. After looking doubtfully at it two or three times, as if to be sure that it was really there, he laid down his work, put his hand to his neck , and took off a blackened string with a scrap of folded rag attached to it. He opened this carefully on his knee, and it contained a very little quantity of hair-- not more than one or two long golden hairs--which he had, in some old day, wound off upon his finger.

He took her hair into his hand again, and looked closely at it. "It is the same. How can it be! When was this! How was it!"

He sank in her arms, and his face dropped on her breast: a sight so touching, yet so terrible in the tremendous wrong and suffering which had gone before it, that the two beholders covered their faces.

When the quiet of the garret had been long undisturbed, and his heaving breast and shaken form had long yielded to the calm that must follow all storms-- emblem to humanity, of the rest and silence into which the the storm called Life must hush at last--they came forward to raise the father and daughter from the ground. He had gradually dropped to the floor, and lay there in a lethargy, worn out. She had nestled down with him, that his head might lie upon her arms. And her hair drooping over him curtained him from the light.

"If, without disturbing him," she said, raising her hand to Mr. Lorry as he stooped over them after repeated blowings of his nose, "all could be arranged for our leaving Paris at once, so that, from the very door, he could be taken away."

"But, consider. Is he fit for the journey?" asked Mr. Lorry.

"More fit for that, I think, than to remain in this city, so dreadful to him. If you will lock the door to secure us from interruption, I do not doubt that you will find him, when you come back, as quiet as you leave him. In any case, I will take care of him until you return, and then we will remove him straight."

Mr. Lorry and Monsieur Defarge had made all ready for the journey, and had brought with them, besides traveling cloaks and wrappers, bread and meat and wine and hot coffee. Monsieur Defarge put his provender and the lamp he carried on the shoemaker's bench, and he and Mr. Lorry roused the captive and assisted him to his feet.

In the submissive way of one long accustomed to obey under coercion, he ate and drank what they gave him to eat and drink and put on the cloak and other wrappings that they gave him to wear. He readily responded to his daughter's drawing her arm through his, and took, and kept, her hand in both his own.

They began to descend, Monsieur Defarge going first with the lamp, Mr. Lorry closing the little procession.

No crowd was about the door. No people were

discernible at any of the many windows. Not even a chance passer-by was in the street. An unnatural silence and desertion reigned there. Only one soul was to be seen and that was Madame Defarge, who leaned against the door-post, knitting, and saw nothing.

The prisoner got into a coach, and his daughter followed him.

Defarge got upon the box and gave the word "To the Barrier!" The postilion cracked his whip, and they clattered away under the feeble over-swinging lamps.

Five years passed since Mr. Lorry visited the garret room in Saint Antoine and escorted Dr. Manette and his daughter back to London.

Tellson's Bank by Temple Bar was an old-fashioned place, even in the year one thousand seven hundred and eighty. It was very small, very dark, very ugly, very incommodious. It was an old-fashioned place, moreover, in the moral attribute that the partners in the House were proud of its smallness, proud of its darkness, proud of its ugliness, proud of its incommodiousness.

Outside Tellson's --never by any means in it, unless called in--was an odd-job man, an occasional porter and messenger who served as the live sign of the house. He was never absent during business hours, unless upon an errand, and then he was represented by his son--a grisly urchin of twelve, who was his express image. People understood that Tellson's, in a stately way, tolerated the odd-job man. His surname was Cruncher, and on the youthful occasion of his renouncing, by proxy, the works of darkness, in the easterly parish church of Houndsditch, he had received the added appellation of Jerry.

Encamped at a quarter before nine, in good time to touch his three-cornered hat to the oldest of men as they passed in to Tellson's, Jerry took up his station on a windy March morning with young Jerry standing by him--when not engaged in making forays through the Bar to inflict bodily and mental injuries of an acute description on passing boys who were small enough for his amiable purpose. Father and son, extremely like each other, looking silently on at the morning traffic in Fleet Street, with their two heads as near to one another as the two eyes of each were, bore a considerable resemblance to a pair of monkeys.

The head of one of the regular indoor clerks attached to Tellson's establishment was put through the door and the word was given:

"Porter wanted!"

"You know the Old Bailey well, no doubt?" said one of the oldest of the clerks to Jerry the messenger.

"Yes sir," returned Jerry, in something of a dogged manner. "I do know the Bailey."

"Just so. And you know Mr. Lorry."

"I know Mr. Lorry, sir, much better than I know the Bailey."

"Very well. Find the door where the witnesses go in, and show the doorkeeper this note for Mr. Lorry. He will then let you in."

As the ancient clerk deliberately folded and superscribed the note, Mr. Cruncher--after surveying him in silence until he came to the blotting paper stage--remarked:

"I suppose they'll be trying forgeries this morning?"

"Treason!"

"Ah, that's quartering," said Jerry. "Barbarous!"

"It is the law," remarked the ancient clerk, turning his surprised spectacles upon him. "It is the law."

They hanged at Tyburn, in those days, so the street outside Newgate had not obtained one infamous notoriety that has since attached to it. But, the Old Bailey was famous as a kind of deadly inn-yard, from which pale travelers set out continually, in carts and coaches, on a violent passage into the other world, traversing some two miles and half of public street and road and shaming few good citizens, if any.

Making his way through the tainted crowd, dispersed up and down this hideous scene of action, with the skill of a man accustomed to make his way quietly, the messenger found the door he sought.

After some delay and demur, the door grudgingly turned on its hinges a very little way and allowed Mr. Jerry Cruncher to squeeze himself into the court.

"What's on?" he asked, in a whisper, of the man he found himself next to.

"Nothing yet."

"What's coming on?"

"The treason case."

Mr. Cruncher's attention was here diverted to the door-keeper whom he saw making his way to Mr. Lorry with the note in his hand. Mr. Lorry sat at a table among the gentlemen in wigs. After some gruff coughing and rubbing of his chin and signing with his hand, Jerry attracted the notice of Mr. Lorry, who had stood up to look for him, and who quietly nodded and sat down again.

Presently, the dock became the central point of interest. Two jailers, who had been standing there went out, and the prisoner was brought in and put to the bar.

Everybody present stared at him. All the human breath in the place rolled at him, like a sea, or a wind or a fire. Eager faces strained round pillars and corners to get a sight of him and spectators in back rows stood up not to miss a hair of him.

The object of all this staring and blaring was a young man of about five-and-twenty, well-grown and well-looking, with a sunburnt cheek and a dark eye. His condition was that of a young gentleman. He was plainly dressed in black or very dark gray, and his hair, which was long and dark, was gathered in a ribbon at the back of his neck--more to be out of his way than for ornament. He bowed to the judge and stood quiet.

"Silence in the court!"

Charles Darnay had yesterday pleaded not guilty to an indictment denouncing him for that he was a false traitor to our serene, illustrious, excellent and so forth, prince, our Lord the King, and by reason of his having, on divers occasions, and by divers means and ways, assisted Louis, the French King, in his wars against our said serene, illustrious, excellent, and so forth.

Over the prisoner's head there was a mirror to throw the light down upon him. Crowds of the wicked and wretched had been reflected in it and had passed from its surface and this earth's together. Be that as it may, a change in his position making him conscious of a bar of light across his face, he looked up. And when he saw the glass his face flushed, and he looked away.

It happened that the action turned his face to that side of the court which was on his left. About on a level with his eyes, there sat, in that corner of the Judge's bench, two persons upon whom his look immediately rested--so immediately, and so much to the changing of his aspect, that all the eyes that were turned upon him, turned to them.

The spectators saw in the two figures, a young lady of little more than twenty, and a gentlemen who was evidently her father: a man of very remarkable appearance in respect of the absolute whiteness of his hair and a certain indescribable intensity of face: not of an active kind, but pondering and self-communing.

Jerry the messenger, who had made his own observations, in his own manner, stretched his neck to hear who they were. The crowd about him had pressed and passed the inquiry on to the nearest attendant, and from him it had been more slowly pressed and passed back. At last it got to Jerry.

"Witnesses,"

"For which side?"

"Against."

"Against what side?"

"The prisoner's."

The Judge, whose eyes had gone in the general direction, recalled them, leaned back in his seat and looked steadily at the man whose life was in his hands as Mr. Attorney-General rose to spin the rope, grind the ax and hammer the nails into the scaffold.

Mr. Attorney-General had to inform the jury that the prisoner before them, though young in years, was old in the treasonable practices which claimed the forfeit of his life. That it was certain, the prisoner had, for longer than that, been in the habit of passing and repassing between France and England on secret business of which he could give no honest account.

That the evidence of two witnesses, coupled with documents of their discovering, would be produced, showing the prisoner to have been furnished with lists of his Majesty's forces and of their disposition and preparation both by sea and land. That these lists could not be proved to be in the prisoner's handwriting. But that it was all the same. That, indeed, it was rather the better for the prosecution, as showing the prisoner to be artful in his precautions. That the proof would go back five years and would show the prisoner already engaged in these pernicious missions, within a few weeks before the date of the very first action fought between the British troops and the Americans. That, for these reasons, the jury being a loyal jury (as he knew they were), and being a responsible jury (as they knew they were), must positively find the prisoner guilty and make an end of him, whether they liked it or not.

(End of Side 1)

When the Attorney-General ceased, a buzz arose in the court as if a cloud of great blue-flies were swarming about the prisoner in anticipation of what he was soon to become. Mr. Attorney-General then called Mr. Jarvis Lorry.

"Mr. Jarvis Lorry, are you a clerk in Tellson's Bank?"

"I am."

"On a certain Friday night in November, one thousand seven hundred and seventy-five, did business occasion you to travel between London and Dover by the mail?"

"It did."

"Where there any other passengers in the mail?"

"Two."

"Did they alight on the road in the course of the night?"

"They did."

"Mr. Lorry, look upon the prisoner. Was he one of those two passengers?"

"I cannot undertake to say that he was."

"Mr. Lorry, look once more upon the prisoner. Have you seen him to your certain knowledge, before?"

"I have."

"When?"

"I was returning from France a few days afterwards, and at Calais the prisoner came on board the packet-ship in which I returned and made the voyage with me."

"At what hour did he come on board?"

"At a little after midnight."

"In the dead of the night. Was he the only passenger who came on board at that untimely hour?"

"He happened to be the only one."

"No mind about 'happening,' Mr. Lorry. He was the only passenger who came on board in the dead of the night?"

"He was."

"Were you traveling alone, Mr. Lorry, or with any companion?"

"With two companions. A gentleman and a lady. They are here."

"They are here. Had you any conversation with the prisoner?"

"Hardly any. The weather was stormy and the passage long and rough, and I lay on a sofa almost from shore to shore."

"Miss Manette!"

The young lady to whom all eyes had been turned before, and were now turned again, stood upon where she had sat. Her father rose with her and kept her hand drawn through his arm.

"Miss Manette, have you seen the prisoner before?"

"Yes, sir."

"Where?"

"On board of the packet-ship just now referred to, sir, and on the same occasion."

"Miss Manette, had you any conversation with the prisoner on that passage across the Channel?"

"Yes, sir."

"Recall it."

"When the prisoner came on board, he noticed that my

father was much fatigued and in a very weak state of health. The prisoner was so good as to beg permission to advise me how I could shelter my father from the wind and weather better than I had done. He expressed great gentleness and kindness for my father's state, and I am sure that he felt it. That was the manner of our beginning to speak together."

"Let me interrupt you for a moment. Had he come on board alone?"

"No."

"How many were with him?"

"Two French gentlemen."

"Had they conferred together?"

"They had conferred together until the last moment, when it was necessary for the French gentlemen to be landed in their boat."

"Now to the prisoner's conversation, Miss Manette."

"The prisoner was as open in his confidence with me--which arose out of my helpless situation--as he was kind and good and useful to my father. I hope," she said, bursting into tears, "I may not repay him by doing him harm today."

Buzzing from the blue-flies.

Mr. Attorney-General now signified to my Lord, that he deemed it necessary, as a matter of precaution and form, to call the young lady's father, Doctor Manette-- who was called accordingly.

"Doctor Manette, look upon the prisoner. Have you ever seen him before?"

"Once. When he called at my lodgings in London. Some three years, or three years and a half ago.'

"Can you identify him as your fellow-passenger on board the packet, or speak of his conversation with your daughter?"

"Sir, I can do neither. My mind is a blank, from sometime--I cannot even say what time--when I employed myself, in my captivity, in making shoes, to the time when I found myself living in London with my dear daughter here. She had become familiar to me, when a gracious God restored my faculties. But, I am quite unable to say how she became familiar. I have no remembrance of the process."

Mr. Attorney-General sat down, and the father and daughter sat down together.

A singular circumstance then arose in the case, the object in hand being to show that the prisoner went down, with some fellow plotter untracked, in the Dover mail on that Friday night in November five years ago and got out of the mail in the night as a blind, at a place where he did not remain, but from which he traveled back some dozen miles or more to a garrison and dockyard and there collected information. A witness was called to identify him as having been at the precise time required in the coffee-room of an hotel in that garrison-and-dockyard town, waiting for another person. The prisoner's counsel was cross-examining this witness with no result, except that he had never seen the prisoner on any other occasion, when a wigged gentleman who had all this time been looking at the ceiling of the court wrote a word or two on a little piece of paper, screwed it up, and tossed it to him. Opening this piece of paper in the next pause, the counsel looked with great attention and curiosity at the prisoner.

"You say again you are quite sure that it was the prisoner?"

The witness was quite sure.

"Did you ever see anybody very like the prisoner?"

Not so like (the witness said) as that he could be mistaken.

"Look well upon that gentleman, my learned friend there," pointing to him who had tossed the paper over, "and then look upon the prisoner. How say you? Are they very like each other?"

Allowing for my learned friend's appearance being careless and slovenly if not debauched, they were sufficiently like each other to surprise not only the witness but everybody present when they were thus brought into comparison. My Lord being prayed to bid my learned friend to lay aside his wig and giving no very gracious consent, the likeness became much more remarkable. My Lord inquired of Mr. Stryver (the prisoner's counsel), whether they were next to try Mr. Carton (name of my learned friend) for treason? The upshot of which was to smash this witness like a crockery vessel and shiver his part of the case to useless lumber.

Mr. Cruncher had by this time taken quite a lunch off his fingers in his following of the evidence. He had now to attend while Mr. Stryver fitted the prisoner's case on the jury like a compact suit of clothes, showing them how the prosecution witness, John Barsad, was a hired spy and traitor, an unblushing trafficker in blood, and one of the greatest scoundrels upon earth since accursed Judas--which he certainly did look rather like. How the second, a Roger Cly, was his friend and partner and was worthy to be. How the watchful eyes of these forgers and false swearers had rested on the prisoner as a victim, because some family affairs in France, he being of French extraction, did require his making those passages across the Channel--

though what those affairs were, a consideration for others who were near and dear to him forbade him even for his life to disclose. Mr. Stryver further showed the jury how the evidence that had been warped and wrested from the young lady, whose anguish in giving it they had witnessed, came to nothing, involving the mere little innocent gallantries and politenesses likely to pass between any young gentleman and young lady so thrown together. The great flies swarmed again.

Mr. Carton, who had so long sat looking at the ceiling of the court, changed neither his place nor his attitude even in this excitement. There was something especially reckless in his demeanor that gave him a disreputable look. Yet, he took in more of the details of the scene than he appeared to take in. For now, when Miss Manette's head dropped upon her father's breast, he was the first to see it and to say audibly: "Officer! look to that young lady. Help the gentleman to take her out. Don't you see, she will fall!"

There was much commiseration for her as she was

removed and much sympathy with her father. It had evidently been a great distress to him to have the days of his imprisonment recalled. He had shown strong internal agitation when he was questioned, and that pondering or brooding look which made him old had been upon him like a heavy cloud ever since. As he passed out, the jury, who had turned back and paused a moment, spoke through their foreman.

They were not agreed and wished to retire. Mr. Lorry, who had gone out when the young lady and her father went out, now reappeared and beckoned to Jerry who in the slackened interest could easily get near him.

"Jerry, if you wish to take something to eat, you can. But, keep in the way. You will be sure to hear when the jury come in. Don't be a moment behind them, for I want you to take the verdict back to the bank. You are the quickest messenger I know and will get to Temple Bar long before I can."

An hour and a half limped heavily away in the thief-and-rascal crowded passages below, even though assisted off with mutton pies and ale. The hoarse messenger, uncomfortably seated on a form after taking that refection, had dropped into a doze, when a loud murmur and a rapid tide of people setting up the stairs that led to the court carried him along with them.

"Jerry, Jerry!" Mr. Lorry was already calling at the door when he got there.

"Here, sir. It's a fight to get back. Here I am, sir!

Mr. Lorry handed him a paper through the throng.

"Quick! Have you got it?"

"Yes, sir."

Hastily written on the paper was the word "Acquitted."

From the dimly-lighted passages of the court, the last sediment of the human stew that had been boiling there all day was straining off when Doctor Manette, Lucie Manette, his daughter, Mr. Lorry, the solicitor for the defense, and its counsel, Mr. Stryver stood gathered round Mr. Charles Darnay, just released, congratulating him on his escape from death.

Mr. Darnay kissed Miss Manette's hand fervently and gratefully and turned to Mr. Stryver, whom he warmly thanked.

The friends of the acquitted prisoner then dispersed. Another person, who had not joined the group or interchanged a word with any one of them, now stepped up and turned to Darnay: "This is a strange chance that throws you and me together. This must be a strange night to you, standing alone here with your counterpart, on these street stones," said Carton.

Nobody had made any acknowledgment of Mr. Carton's part in the day's proceedings. Nobody had known of it.

"I hardly seem yet," returned Charles Darnay, "to belong to this world again."

"I don't wonder at it. It's not so long since you were pretty far advanced on your way to another. You speak faintly."

"I begin to think I am faint."

"Then why the devil don't you dine? I dined,

myself, while those numbskulls were deliberating which world you should belong to--this, or some other. Let me show you the nearest tavern to dine well at."

Drawing his arm through his own, Sydney Carton took him down Ludgate Hill to Fleet Street, and so up a covered way into a tavern. Here, they were shown into a little room where Charles Darnay was soon recruiting his strength with a good plain dinner and good wine--while Carton sat opposite to him at the same table, with his separate bottle of port before him and his fully half-insolent manner upon him.

"Well, now your dinner is done," Carton presently said, "why don't you call a health, Mr. Darnay. Why don't you give a toast?"

"What health? What toast?"

"Why, it's on the tip of your tongue. It ought to be. It must be. I'll swear it's there."

"Miss Manette, then!"

"Miss Manette, then!"

Looking his companion full in the face while he

drank the toast, Carton flung his glass over his shoulder against the wall, where it shivered to pieces.

"That's a fair lady to be pitied by and wept for by! How does it feel? Is it worth being tried for one's life to be the object of such sympathy and compassion, Mr. Darnay?"

Darnay answered not a word.

"Mr. Darnay, let me ask you a question."

"Willingly."

"Do you think I particularly like you?"

"Really, Mr. Carton," returned the other, oddly disconcerted, "I have not asked myself the question."

"But ask yourself the question now."

"You have acted as if you do. But I don't think you do."

"I don't think I do," said Carton. "I begin to have a very good opinion of your understanding."

"Nevertheless," pursued Darnay, rising to ring the bell, "there is nothing in that, I hope, to prevent my calling the reckoning and our parting without ill-blood on either side."

The bill being paid, Charles Darnay rose and wished him good-night. Without returning the wish, Carton rose too, with something of a threat of defiance in his manner, and said, "A last word, Mr. Darnay. You think I am drunk?"

"I think you have been drinking, Mr. Carton."

"Think? You know I have been drinking."

"Since I must say so, I know it."

"Then you shall likewise know why. I am a disappointed drudge, sir. I care for no man on earth, and no man on earth cares for me."

"Much to be regretted. You might have used your talents better."

"Maybe so, Mr. Darnay; maybe not. Don't let your sober face elate you, however. You don't know what it may come to. Good-night!"

When he was left alone, this strange being took up a candle and went to a glass that hung upon the wall.

"Do you particularly like the man?" he muttered, at

his own image. Why should you particularly like a man who resembles you? There is nothing in you to like. You know that. Change places with him, and would you have been looked at by those blue eyes as he was? Come on and have it out in plain words! You hate the fellow."

He resorted to a pint of wine for consolation, drank it all in a few minutes and fell asleep on his arms, with his hair straggling over the table and a long winding sheet in the candle dripping down upon him.

The quiet lodgings of Doctor Manette were in a quiet street-corner not far from Soho Square. On the afternoon of a certain fine Sunday, when the waves of four months had rolled over the trial for treason and carried it, as to the public interest and memory, far out to sea, Mr. Jarvis Lorry walked along the sunny streets from Clerkenwell, where he lived, on his way to dine with the Doctor. After several relapses into business-absorption, Mr. Lorry had become the Doctor's friend, and the quiet street-corner was the sunny part of his life.

Doctor Manette received such patients here as his old reputation, and its revival in the floating whispers of his story, brought him. His scientific knowledge, and his vigilance and skill in conducting ingenious experiments brought him otherwise into moderate request, and he earned as much as he wanted.

These things were within Mr. Jarvis Lorry's knowledge, thoughts, and notice, when he rang the door-bell of the tranquil house in the corner on the fine Sunday afternoon.

"Doctor Manette at home?"

Expected home.

"Miss Lucie at home?"

Expected home.

"Miss Pross at home?"

Possibly at home, but, of a certainty, impossible for handmaid to anticipate intentions of Miss Pross as to admission or denial of the fact.

"As I am at home myself," said Mr. Lorry, "I'll go

upstairs."

There were three rooms on a floor. The first was the best room, and in it were Lucie's birds, and flowers, and books, and desk, and work-table, and a box of water-colors. The second was the Doctor's consulting room, used also as the dining-room; the third, changingly speckled by the rustle of the plane-tree in the yard, was the Doctor's bedroom. And there, in a corner stood the disused shoemaker's bench and tray of tools, much as it had stood on the fifth floor of the dismal house by the wine-shop, in the suburb of Saint Antoine, in Paris.

"I wonder," said Mr. Lorry, pausing in his looking about, "that he keeps that reminder of his sufferings about him!"

"And why wonder at that?" was the abrupt inquiry that made him start.

It proceeded from Miss Pross, the wild, red woman, strong of hand, whose acquaintance he had first made at the Royal George Hotel at Dover and had since improved.

"As we happen to be alone for the moment and are both people of business," Mr. Lorry said, "let me ask you--does the Doctor, in talking with Lucie, never refer to the shoemaking time, yet?'

"Never."

"And yet keeps that bench and those tools beside him?"

"Ah!" returned Miss Pross, shaking her head. "But I don't say he don't refer to it within himself."

"Do you believe that he thinks of it much?"

"I do," said Miss Pross.

"Do you imagine--" Mr. Lorry had begun, when Miss Pross took him up short.

"Here they are," said she, rising to break up the conference.

Miss Pross was a pleasant sight, albeit wild and red and grim, taking off her darling's bonnet when she came upstairs, and touching it up with the ends of her handkerchief, and blowing the dust off it, and folding her mantle ready for laying by, and smoothing her rich hair with as much pride as she could possibly have taken in her own hair if she had been the vainest and handsomest of women.

On Sundays, Miss Pross dined at the Doctor's table, but on other days persisted in taking her meals at unknown periods, either in the lower regions, or in her own room on the second floor.

It was an oppressive day, and after dinner Lucie proposed that the wine should be carried out under the plane-tree, and they should sit there in the air.

Shortly, Mr. Darnay presented himself while they were sitting under the plane tree. Doctor Manette received him kindly, and so did Lucie. But, Miss Pross suddenly became afflicted with a twitching in the head and body and retired into the house. She was not unfrequently the victim of this disorder, and she called it in familiar conversation, "a fit of the jerks."

The Doctor was in his best condition and looked especially young. The resemblance between him and Lucie was very strong at such times, and as they sat side by side, she leaning on his shoulder and he resting his arm on the back of her chair, it was very agreeable to trace the likeness.

Tea-time, and Miss Pross making tea, with another fit of the jerks upon her since Mr. Carton had lounged in.

The night was so very sultry that although they sat with doors and windows open, they were overpowered by heat. When the tea-table was done with, they all moved to one of the windows and looked out into the heavy twilight. Lucie sat by her father and Darnay sat beside her and Carton leaned against a window. The curtains were long and white, and some of the thunder gusts that whirled into the corner from the approaching storm caught them up to the ceiling and waved them like spectral wings.

"The rain-drops are still falling, large, heavy and few," said Doctor Manette. "It comes slowly."

"It comes surely," said Carton.

They spoke low, as people watching and waiting

mostly do; as people in a dark room, watching and waiting for lightning, always do.

Monseigneur, one of the great lords in power at the Court, held his fortnightly reception in his grand hotel in Paris. Monseigneur was in his inner room, his sanctuary of sanctuaries, his Holiest of Holiests, to the crowd of worshipers in the suite of rooms without. Monseigneur was about to take his chocolate.

It took four men, all four ablaze with gorgeous decorations to conduct the happy chocolate to Monseigneur's lips. One lackey carried the chocolate-pot into the sacred presence. A second milled and frothed the chocolate with the little instrument he bore for that function. A third presented the favored napkin. A fourth poured the chocolate out. It was impossible for Monseigneur to dispense with one of these attendants on the chocolate and hold his high place under the admiring Heavens.

It seemed that the leprosy of unreality disfigured every human creature in attendance upon Monseigneur.

But, the comfort was that all the company at the grand hotel of Monseigneur were perfectly dressed. If the Day of Judgment had only been ascertained to be a dress day, everybody there would have been eternally correct.

Dress was the one unfailing talisman and charm used for keeping all things in their places.

Monseigneur, having eased his four men of their burdens and taken his chocolate, caused the doors of the Holiest of Holiests to be thrown open and issued forth. Then what submission, what cringing and fawning what servility, what abject humiliation!

Bestowing a word of promise here and a smile there, a whisper on one happy slave and a wave of the hand on another, Monseigneur affably passed through his rooms.

The show being over, there was soon but one person left, of all the crowd, and he, with his hat under his arm and his snuffbox in his hand, slowly passed among the mirrors on his way out.

"I devote you," said this person, stopping at the last door on his way, and turning in the direction of the sanctuary, "to the Devil."

With that, he shook the snuff from his fingers as if he had shaken the dust from his feet and quietly walked downstairs.

He was a man of about sixty, handsomely dressed, haughty in manner and with a face like a fine mask: a face of transparent paleness, every feature in it clearly defined, one set expression on it. The man went downstairs into the courtyard, got into his carriage and drove away.

Not many people had talked with him at the reception. He had stood in a little space apart and Monseigneur might have been warmer in his manner. It appeared, under the circumstances, rather agreeable to him to see the common people dispersed before his horses and often barely escaping from being run down. His man drove as if he were charging an enemy. And the furious recklessness of the man brought no check into the face or to the lips of the master.

With a wild rattle and clatter and an inhuman

abandonment of consideration, not easy to be understood in these days, the carriage dashed through the streets and swept round corners, with women screaming before it, and men clutching each other and clutching children out of its way. At last, swooping at a street corner by a fountain, one of its wheels came to a sickening little jolt. There was a loud cry from a number of voices, and the horses reared and plunged. But for the latter inconvenience, the carriage probably would not have stopped. Carriages were often known to drive on and leave their wounded behind. And why not? But, the frightened valet had got down in a hurry, and there were twenty hands at the horses' bridles.

"What has gone wrong?" said monsieur, calmly looking out.

The tall man in the nightcap had caught up a bundle from among the feet of the horses and had laid it on the base of the fountain and was down in the mud and wet howling over it like a wild animal.

"Pardon, monsieur the marquis!" said a ragged and

submissive man, "it is a child."

"Why does he make that abominable noise? Is it his child?"

"Excuse me, monsieur the marquis--it is a pity--yes."

Monsieur the marquis, took out his purse. "It is extraordinary to me," said he, "that you people cannot take care of yourselves and your children. One or the other of you is forever in the way. How do I know what injury you have done my horses? See, give him that." He threw out a gold coin for the valet to pick up, and all the heads craned forward that all the eyes might look down at it as it fell.

The tall man called out again with a most unearthly cry, "Dead!"

Without deigning to look at the assemblage a second time, monsieur the marquis leaned back in his seat and was just being driven away with the air of a gentleman who had accidentally broken some common thing and had paid for it, and could afford to pay for it, when his ease was suddenly disturbed by a coin flying into his carriage and ringing on its floor.

"Hold," said monsieur the marquis, "Hold the horses! Who threw that? You dogs," said the marquis, "I would ride over any one of you very willingly and exterminate you from the earth. If I knew which rascal threw at the carriage and if that brigand were sufficiently near it, he should be crushed under the wheels."

So cowed was their condition, and so long and hard their experience of what such a man could do to them, within the law and beyond it, that not a voice or a hand or even an eye was raised--among the men, not one. But one woman who stood knitting looked up steadily, and looked the marquis in the face. It was not for his dignity to notice it. His contemptuous eyes passed over her and over all the other rats, and he leaned back in his seat again and gave the word "Go on!"

It was a heavy mass of building, that chateau of monsieur the marquis, with a large stone courtyard before it, and two stone sweeps of staircase meeting in a stone terrace before the principal door--a stony business altogether, with heavy stone balustrades, and stone urns, and stone flowers, and stone faces of men, and stone heads of lions in all directions, as if the Gorgon's head had surveyed it when it was finished two centuries ago.

The great door clanged behind him, and monsieur the marquis crossed a hall grim with certain old boar-spears, swords, and knives of the chase; grimmer with certain heavy riding-rods and riding-whips, of which many a peasant gone to his benefactor Death had felt the weight when his lord was angry.

"My nephew, Monsieur Charles, whom I expect, is he arrived from England?"

"Monseigneur, not yet," a humble voice replied.

"Ah, it is not probable he will arrive tonight. Nevertheless, leave the table as it is. I shall be ready in a quarter of an hour."

In a quarter of an hour, the marquis was ready and sat down alone to his sumptuous and choice supper. He was half-way through it when he again stopped with his glass in his hand, hearing the sound of wheels. It came on briskly and came up to the front of the chateau.

"Ask who has arrived."

It was his nephew. He was to be told, said the marquis, that supper awaited him then and there and that he was prayed to come to it. In a little while he came. He had been known in England as Charles Darnay. The marquis received him in a courtly manner, but they did not shake hands.

"You left Paris yesterday, sir?" he said, to the marquis as he took his seat at the table.

"Yesterday. And you?"

"I come direct."

"From London?"

"Yes."

"You have been a long time coming," said the marquis with a smile.

"On the contrary, I come direct."

"Pardon me, I mean not a long time on the journey--a

long time intending the journey."

"I have been detained by," the nephew stopped a moment in his answer, "various business."

"Without doubt," said the polished uncle.

So long as a servant was present, no other words passed between them. When coffee had been served and they were alone together, the nephew, looking at the uncle and meeting the eyes of the face that was like a fine mask, opened the conversation.

"There is not," he said, "a face I can look at in all this country round about us which looks at me with any deference on it but the dark deference of fear and slavery."

"A compliment," said the marquis, "to the grandeur of the family, merited by the manner in which the family has sustained its grandeur. Repression is the only lasting philosophy."

"The dark deference of fear and slavery, my friend," observed the marquis, "will keep the dogs obedient to the whip as long as this roof shuts out the sky.

Meanwhile," continued the marquis, "I will preserve the honor and repose of the family if you will not. But you must be fatigued. Shall we terminate our conference for the night?"

"A moment more."

"An hour if you please."

"Sir," said the nephew, "we have done wrong and are reaping the fruits of wrong."

"We have done wrong?" repeated the marquis, with an inquiring smile and delicately pointing first to his nephew, then to himself.

"Our family," continued Charles, "our honorable family, whose honor is of so much account to both of us, in such different ways--even in my father's time, we did a world of wrong, injuring every human creature who came between us and our pleasure, whatever it was. Why need I speak of my father's time, when it is equally yours? Can I separate my father's twin brother, joint inheritor and next successor, from himself?"

"Death has done that!" said the marquis.

"And has left me," answered the nephew, "bound to a system that is frightful to me. This property and France are lost to me. I renounce them."

"Forgive my curiosity," said the uncle, "do you, under your new philosophy, graciously intend to live?"

"I must do, to live what others of my countrymen, even with nobility at their backs, may have to do someday. Work!"

"In England, for example?"

"Yes. The family honor, sir, is safe from me in this country. The family name can suffer from me and no other, for I bear it in no other."

"England is very attractive to you, seeing how indifferently you have prospered there," observed the Marquis, turning his calm face to his nephew, with a smile.

"Good night! I look to the pleasure of seeing you again in the morning. Good repose! Light monsieur my nephew to his chamber there! And burn monsieur my nephew in his bed, if you will," he added to himself, before he rang his little bell again and summoned his valet to his own bedroom.

For several heavy hours, the stone faces of the chateau, lion and human, stared blindly at the night.

The fountain in the village flowed unseen and unheard, and the fountain at the chateau dropped unseen and unheard. Then the gray water of both began to be ghostly in the light, and the eyes of the stone faces of the chateau were opened.

Lighter and lighter, until at last the sun touched the tops of the still trees and poured its radiance over the hill.

Now, the sun was full up, and movement began in the village. Casement windows opened, crazy doors were unbarred, and people came forth shivering, chilled, as yet, by the new sweet air.

These trivial incidents belonged to the routine of life and the return of morning. Surely not so the ringing of the great bell of the chateau, nor the running up and down the stairs, nor the hurried figures on the terrace, nor the booting and tramping here and there and everywhere, nor the quick saddling of horses and riding away.

What did all this portend, and what portended the swift hoisting-up of Monsieur Gabelle who is the postmaster and tax collector of the town behind a servant on horseback, and the conveying away of the said Gabelle (double-laden though the horse was), at a gallop?

It portended that there was one stone face too many, up at the chateau.

The Gorgon had surveyed the building again in the night and had added the one stone face wanting; the stone face for which it had waited through about two hundred years.

It lay back on the pillow of monsieur the marquis. It was like a fine mask, suddenly startled, made angry and petrified. Driven home into the heart of the stone figure attached to it, was a knife. Round its hilt was a frill of paper, on which was scrawled:

"Drive him fast to his tomb. This, from Jacques."

More months, to the number of twelve, had come and gone, and Mr. Charles Darnay was established in England as a higher teacher of the French language who was conversant with French literature.

He had loved Lucie Manette from the hour of his danger. He had never heard a sound so sweet and dear as the sound of her compassionate voice. He had never seen a face so tenderly beautiful as hers was when it was confronted with his own on the edge of the grave that had been dug for him. But, he had not yet spoken to her on the subject. The assassination at the deserted chateau far away beyond the heaving water and the long, long, dusty roads--the solid stone chateau which had itself become the mere mist of a dream--had been done a year. And he had never yet, by so much as a single spoken word, disclosed to her the state of his heart.

That he had his reasons for this, he knew full well. It was again a summer day when, lately arrived in London from his college occupation, he turned into the quiet corner in Soho, bent on seeking an opportunity of opening his mind to Doctor Manette. It was the close of the summer day, and he knew Lucie to be out with Miss Pross.

He found the Doctor reading in his armchair at a window.

"Charles Darnay! I rejoice to see you. We have been counting on your return these three or four days past. Mr. Stryver and Sydney Carton were both here yesterday, and both made you out to be more than due."

"I am obliged to them for their interest in the matter," he answered, a little coldly as to them though very warmly as to the Doctor. "Miss Manette--"

"Is well," said the Doctor, as he stopped short, "and your return will delight us all. She has gone out on some household matters and will soon be home."

"Doctor Manette, I knew she was from home. I took the opportunity of her being from home to beg to speak to you."

"Is Lucie the topic?"

"She is."

"It is hard for me to speak of her at any time. It is very hard for me to hear her spoken of in that tone of yours, Charles Darnay."

"It is a tone of fervent admiration, true homage, and deep love, Doctor Manette!" he said deferentially.

"Have you spoken to Lucie?"

"No."

"Nor written?"

"Never."

"It would be ungenerous to affect, not to know, that your self-denial is to be referred to your consideration for her father. Her father thanks you."

He offered his hand, but his eyes did not go with it.

"I know," said Darnay, respectfully. "How can I fail to know, Doctor Manette--I, who have seen you together from day to day--that between you and Miss Manette there is an affection so unusual, so touching, so belonging to the circumstances in which it has been nurtured, and that it can have few parallels even in the tenderness between a father and child.

"You speak so feelingly and so manfully, Charles Darnay, that I thank you with all my heart, and will open all my heart--or nearly so. Have you any reason to believe that Lucie loves you?"

"None. As yet, none."

"Is it the immediate object of this confidence, that you may at once ascertain that, with my knowledge?"

"Not even so. I might not have the hopefulness to do it for weeks; I might (mistaken or not mistaken) have that hopefulness tomorrow."

"Do you seek any guidance from me?"

"May I ask, sir, if you think she is--" As he hesitated, her father supplied the rest.

"Is she sought by any other suitor?"

"It is what I meant to say."

Her father considered a little before he answered:

"You have seen Mr. Carton here yourself. Mr. Stryver is here too, occasionally. If it be at all, it can only be by one of these."

"Or both," said Darnay. Then he continued, "Your confidence in me ought be returned with full confidence on my part. My present name, though but slightly changed from my mother's, is not, as you will remember, my own. I wish to tell you what it is and why I am in England."

"Stop!" said the doctor of Beauvais.

"I wish it, that I may the better deserve your confidence, and have no secret from you.

"Stop!" For an instant, the Doctor even had his two hands at his ears, for another instant even had his two hands laid on Darnay's lips.

"Tell me when I ask you, not now. If your suit should prosper, if Lucie should love you, you shall tell me on your marriage morning. Do you promise?"

"Willingly."

"Give me your hand. She will be home directly, and it is better she should not see us together tonight. Go! God bless you!"

If Sydney Carton ever shone anywhere, he certainly never shone in the house of Doctor Manette. He had been there often, during a whole year, and had always been the same moody and morose lounger there.

However, on a day in August, his feet became animated by an intention, and in the working out of that intention, they took him to the Doctor's door. He was shown upstairs and found Lucie at her work alone. She had never been quite at her ease with him and received him with some little embarrassment as he seated himself near her table. But looking up at his face in the interchange of the first few common places, she observed a change in him.

"I fear you are not well, Mr. Carton."

"No, but the life I lead, Miss Manette, is not conducive to health. What is to be expected of or by, such profligates?"

"Is it not--oh, forgive me, I have begun the question on my lips--a pity to live no better life?"

"God knows, it is a shame."

"Then why not change it?"

Looking gently at him again, she was surprised and saddened to see that there were tears in his eyes. There were tears in his voice, too, as he answered:

"It is too late for that. I shall never be better than I am I am to sink lower and be worse. Pray, forgive me, Miss Manette, I break down before the knowledge of what I am about to say to you. Will you hear me?"

"If it will do you any good, Mr. Carton. If it would make you any happier, it would make me very glad."

"God bless you for your sweet compassion."

He unshaded his face, after a little while and spoke steadily.

(End of Side 2)

"If it had been possible, Miss Manette, that you could have returned the love of the man that you see before you--self flung away, wasted, drunken, poor creature of misuse as you know him to be--he would have been conscious this day and hour,in spite of his happiness, that he would bring you to misery, bring you to sorrow and repentance, blight you, disgrace you, pull you down with him. I know very well that you can have no tenderness for me. I ask for none. I am even thankful that it cannot be.

"Without it, can I not save you, Mr. Carton? Can I not recall you--forgive me again!--to a better course? Can I in no way repay your confidence? I know this is a confidence," she modestly said after a little hesitation, and in earnest tears. "I know you would say this to no one else. Can I turn it to no good account for yourself, Mr. Carton?"

He shook his head.

"My last supplication of all is this: try to hold me in your mind, at some quiet times, as ardent and sincere in this one thing. The time will come, the time will not be long in coming, when new ties will be formed about you, ties that will bind you yet more tenderly and strongly to the home you so adorn--the dearest ties that will ever grace and gladden you. Oh, Miss Manette, when the little picture of a happy father's face looks up in yours, when you see your own bright beauty springing up anew at your feet, think now and then that there is a man who would give his life to keep a life you love beside you!

He said, "Farewell!" said, a last "God Bless you!" and left her.

Never did the sun go down with a brighter glory on the quiet corner in Soho than one memorable evening when the doctor and his daughter sat under the plane-tree together. Never did the moon rise with a milder radiance over great London than on that night when it found them still seated under the tree and shone upon their faces through its leaves.

Lucie was to be married tomorrow. She had reserved

this last evening for her father, and they sat alone under the plane-tree.

"You are happy, my dear father?'

"Quite, my child."

They had said little though they had been there a long time. When it was yet light enough to work and read, she had neither engaged herself in her usual work, nor had she read to him. She had employed herself in both ways at his side under the tree many and many a time. But this time was not quite like any other, and nothing could make it so.

"And I am very happy tonight dear father. I am deeply happy in the love that Heaven has so blessed--my love for Charles, and Charles's love for me. But if my life were not to be still consecrated to you, or if my marriage were so arranged as that it would part us, even by the length of a few of these streets, I should be more unhappy and self-reproachful now than I can tell you. He embraced her, solemnly commended her to Heaven, and humbly thanked Heaven for having bestowed her on him. By and by, they went into the house.

There was no one bidden to the marriage but Mr. Lorry. There was even to be no bridesmaid but the gaunt Miss Pross.

The marriage day was shining brightly, and they were ready outside the closed door of the doctor's room, where he was speaking with Charles Darnay. They were ready to go to church: the beautiful bride, Mr. Lorry and Miss Pross.

The door of the doctor's room opened, and he came out with Charles Darnay. He was so deadly pale--which had not been the case when they went in together--that no vestige of color was to be seen in his face. But in the composure of his manner he was unaltered, except, that to the shrewd glance of Mr. Lorry, it disclosed some shadowy indication that the old air of avoidance and dread had lately passed over him like a cold wind.

He gave his arm to his daughter and took her downstairs to the chariot which Mr. Lorry had hired in honor of the day. The rest followed in another carriage, and soon, in a neighboring church where no strange eyes looked on, Charles Darnay and Lucie Manette were happily married.

When the newly married pair came home, the first person who appeared to offer his congratulations was Sydney Carton. He was not improved in habits, or in looks, or in manner, but there was a certain rugged air of fidelity about him which was new to the observation of Charles Darnay.

He watched his opportunity of taking Darnay aside into a window and of speaking to him when no one overheard.

"Mr. Darnay," said Carton. "I wish we might be friends."

"We are already friends, I hope."

"You are good enough to say so, as a fashion of speech. But, I don't mean any fashion of speech. Indeed, when I say I wish we might be friends, I scarcely mean quite that either."

Charles Darnay, as was natural, asked him, in all

good-humor and good-fellowship, what he did mean?

"Upon my life," said Carton, smiling, "I find that easier to comprehend in my own mind than to convey to yours. However, let me try. You remember a certain famous occasion when I was more drunk than--than usual?

"I remember a certain famous occasion when you forced me to confess that you had been drinking."

"Yes, I remember it too. The curse of those occasions is heavy upon me, for I always remember them. I hope it may be taken into account one day, when all days are at an end for me! Don't be alarmed. I am not going to preach."

"I am not at all alarmed. Earnestness in you is anything but alarming to me."

"Ah!" said Carton, with a careless wave of his hand, as if he waved that away. "On the drunken occasion in question (one of a large number, as you know), I was insufferable about liking you and not liking you. I wish you would forget it."

"I forgot it long ago." They shook hands upon it,

and Sydney turned away. Within in a minute, he was, to all outward appearance, as unsubstantial as ever.

When he was gone, and in the course of an evening passed with Miss Pross, the Doctor, and Mr. Lorry, Charles Darnay made some mention of this conversation, in general terms, and spoke of Sydney Carton as a problem of carelessness and recklessness. He spoke of him, in short, not bitterly or meaning to bear hard upon him, but as anybody might who saw him as he showed himself.

He had no idea that this could dwell in the thoughts of his fair young wife. But, when he afterwards joined her in their own rooms, he found her waiting for him with the old pretty lifting of the forehead strongly marked.

"We are thoughtful tonight!" said Darnay, drawing his arm about her.

"Yes, dearest Charles," with her hand on his breast, and the inquiring and attentive expression fixed upon him. "We are rather thoughtful tonight, for we have something on our mind tonight."

"What is it, my Lucie?"

"Will you promise not to press one question on me, if I beg you not to ask it?"

"Will I promise? What will I not promise to my love?" What, indeed, with his hand putting aside the golden hair from the cheek, and his other hand against the heart that beat for him!

"I think, Charles, poor Mr. Carton deserves more consideration and respect than you expressed for him tonight.

"Indeed, my own? Why so?"

"That is what you are not to ask me! But I think--I know--he does.   And, oh my dearest love!" she urged clinging nearer to him, laying her head upon his breast and raising her eyes to his, "remember how strong we are in our happiness and how weak he is in his misery!"

The supplication touched him home. "I will always remember it, dear heart! I will remember it as long as I live."

Ever busily winding the golden thread which bound her husband and her father and herself and her old directress and companion in a life of quiet bliss, Lucie sat in the still house in the tranquilly resounding corner listening to the echoing footsteps of years.

Time passed and her little Lucie lay on her bosom. Then among the advancing echoes there was the tread of her tiny feet and the sound of her prattling words. The shady house was sunny with a child's laugh, and the divine friend of children, to whom in her trouble she has confided hers, seemed to take her child in his arms --as he took the child of old, and made it a sacred joy to her. Little Lucie, comically studious at the task of the morning, or dressing a doll at her mother's footstool, chatted in the tongues of the two cities that were blended in her life.

The echoes rarely answered to the actual tread of Sydney Carton. Some half dozen times a year, at most, he claimed his privilege of coming in uninvited and would sit among them through the evening as he had once done often. He never came there heated with wine. And one other thing regarding him was whispered in the echoes, which has been whispered by all true echoes for ages and ages.

No man ever really loved a woman, lost her, and knew her with a blameless though an unchanged mind when she was wife and a mother, but her children had a strange sympathy with him--an instinctive delicacy of pity for him. What fine hidden sensibilities are touched in such a case, no echoes tell, but it is so, and it was so here. Carton was the first stranger to whom little Lucie held out her chubby arms, and he kept his place with her as she grew.

But there were other echoes, from a distance that rumbled menacingly in the corner all through this space of time. And it was now about little Lucie's sixth birthday that they began to have an awful sound, as of a great storm in France with a dreadful sea rising.

The Paris suburb of Saint Antoine had been, that morning, a vast dusky mass of scarecrows, heaving to and fro with frequent gleams of light above the billowy heads, where steel blades and bayonets shone in the sun.

As a whirlpool of boiling waters has a center point, so all this raging circled round Defarge's wine-shop. And every human drop in the caldron had a tendency to be sucked towards the vortex where Defarge himself, already begrimed with gunpowder and sweat, issued orders, issued arms, thrust this man back, dragged this man forward, disarmed one to arm another, labored and strove in the thickest of the uproar.

"Keep near to me, Jacques Three," cried Defarge; "and do you, Jacques One and Two, separate and put yourselves at the head of as many of these patriots as you can. Where is my wife?"

"Eh, well! Here you see me!" said Madame, composed as ever, but not knitting today. Madame's resolute right hand was occupied with an ax, in place of the usual softer implements, and in her girdle were a pistol and a cruel knife.

"Where do you go, my wife?"

"I go," said Madame, "with you at present. You shall see me at the head of women, by and by."

"Come then!" cried Defarge, in a resounding voice. "Patriots and friends, we are ready! The Bastille!"

With a roar that sounded as if all the breath in France had been shaped into the detested word, the living sea rose, wave on wave, depth on depth, and overflowed the city to that point. Alarm bells ringing, drums beating, the sea raging and thundering on its new beach, the attack began.

Deep ditches, double drawbridge, massive stone walls, eight great towers, cannon, muskets, fire and smoke. Through the fire and through the smoke--in the fire and in the smoke, for the sea cast him up against a cannon and on the instant he became a cannoneer--Defarge of the wine-shop worked like a manful soldier, two fierce hours.

A white flag from within the fortress, and a parley --this dimly perceptible through the raging storm, nothing audible in it--suddenly the sea rose immeasurably wider and higher, and swept Defarge of the wine-shop over the lowered drawbridge, past the massive stone outer walls, in among the eight great towers. Surrendered!

So resistless was the force of the ocean bearing him on, that even to draw his breath or turn his head was as impracticable, as if he had been struggling in the surf at the South Sea, until he was landed in the outer courtyard of the Bastille. There, against an angle of a wall, he made a struggle to look about him. Jacques Three was nearly at his side. Madame Defarge, still heading some of her women, was visible in the inner distance, and her knife was in her hand. Everywhere was tumult, exultation, deafening and maniacal bewilderment, astounding noise, yet furious dumb-show.

"The prisoners!"

"The records!"

"The secret cells!"

"The instruments of torture!"

"The prisoners!"

Of all these cries, and ten thousand incoherencies, "The prisoners!" was the cry most taken up by the sea that rushed in, as if there were an eternity of people as well as of time and space.

The hour was come when Saint Antoine was to execute its horrible idea of hoisting up men for lamps, to show what it could be and do. Saint Antoine's blood was up, and the blood of tyranny and domination by the iron hand was down--down on the steps of the Hotel de Ville where the governor's body lay, down on the sole of the shoe of Madame Defarge where she had trodden on the body to steady it for mutilation. "Lower the lamp yonder!" cried Saint Antoine, after glaring round for a new means of death. "Here is one of his soldiers to be left on guard!" The swinging sentinel was posted, and the sea rushed on.

There was a change on the village where the fountain fell. Far and wide lay a ruined country, yielding nothing but desolation.

For scores of years gone by, Monsieur the Marquis,

had squeezed it and wrung it and had seldom graced it with his presence except for the pleasures of the chase.

On one particular evening, when the village had taken its poor supper, it did not creep to bed as it usually did, but came out of doors again and remained there. A curious contagion of whispering was upon it, and also, when it gathered together at the fountain in the dark, another curious contagion of looking expectantly at the sky in one direction only. Monsieur Gabelle, chief functionary of the place, became uneasy, went out on his housetop alone, and looked in that direction too, glanced down from behind his chimneys at the darkening faces by the fountain below, and sent word to the sacristan who kept the keys of the church that there might be need to ring the tocsin, by and by.

The night deepened. The trees environing the old chateau, keeping its solitary state apart, moved in a rising wind as though they threatened the pile of building massive and dark in the gloom.

Presently, the chateau began to make itself

strangely visible by some light of its own as though it were glowing luminous. Then, a flickering streak played behind the architecture of the front, picking out transparent places, and showing where balustrades, arches, and windows were. Then it soared higher and grew broader and brighter. Soon, from a score of the great windows, flames burst forth, and the stone faces awakened, stared out of the fire.

The chateau was left to itself to flame and burn. In the roaring and raging of the conflagration, a red-hot wind, driving straight from the infernal regions, seemed to be blowing the edifice away. With the rising and falling of the blaze, the stone faces showed as if they were in torment.

The village, light-headed with famine, fire, and bell-ringing, and bethinking itself that Monsieur Gabelle had to do with the collection of rent and taxes --though it was but a small installment of taxes, and no rent at all, that Gabelle had got in those latter days-- became impatient for an interview with him, and, surrounding his house, summoned him to come forth for personal conference. Whereupon, Monsieur Gabelle did heavily bar his door and retire to hold counsel with himself.

Probably, Monsieur Gabelle passed a long night up there, with the distant chateau for fire and candle and the beating at his door combined with the joy-ringing, for music. The friendly dawn appeared at last, and as the rush-candles of the village guttered out, the people happily dispersed. Monsieur Gabelle came down, bringing his life with him for that while.

Within a hundred miles, and in the light of other fires, there were other functionaries less fortunate, that night and other nights, whom the rising sun found hanging across once peaceful streets where they had been born and bred.

In such risings of fire and risings of sea--the firm earth shaken by the rushes of an angry ocean which had now no ebb, but was always on the flow, higher and higher, to the terror and wonder of the beholders on the shore--three years of tempest were consumed. Three more birthdays of little Lucie had been woven by the golden thread into the peaceful tissue of the life of her home.

On a steaming, misty afternoon, in the August of the year one thousand seven hundred and ninety-two, Mr. Lorry sat at his desk at Tellson's Bank, and Charles Darnay stood leaning on it, talking with him in a low voice. It was within half an hour or so of the time of closing.

"But although you are the youngest man that ever lived," said Charles Darnay, rather hesitating, "I must still suggest to you--"

"I understand, that I am too old?" said Mr. Lorry.

"Unsettled weather, a long journey, uncertain means of traveling, a disorganized country, a city that may not be safe, even for you."

"My dear Charles," said Mr. Lorry, with a cheerful confidence, "it is safe enough for me. Nobody will care to interfere with an old fellow of hard upon fourscore when there are so many people there much better worth interfering with."

"I wish I were going myself," said Charles Darnay, somewhat restlessly and like one thinking aloud.

"Indeed! You are a pretty fellow to object and advise!" exclaimed Mr. Lorry. "You wish you were going yourself? And you a Frenchman born? Ha! You are a wise counselor."

"However, I am not going," said Charles Darnay, with a smile. "It is more to the purpose that you say you are."

"And I am, in plain reality. The truth is, my dear Charles, you can have no conception of the difficulty with which our business is transacted, and of the peril in which our books and papers in Paris are involved."

"And do you really go tonight?"

"I really go tonight, for the case has become too pressing to admit of delay."

"And do you take no one with you?"

"All sorts of people have been proposed to me, but I will have nothing to say to any of them. I intend to take Jerry. Jerry has been my body-guard on Sunday nights for a long time past, and I am used to him. Nobody will suspect Jerry of being anything but an English bulldog, or of having any design in his head but to fly at anybody who touches his master."

"I must say again that I heartily admire your gallantry and youthfulness."

"I must say again, nonsense, nonsense! When I have executed this little commission, I shall, perhaps, accept Tellson's proposal to retire and live at my ease. Time enough, then, to think about growing old."

At that moment, a messenger approached Mr. Lorry, and laying a soiled and unopened letter before him, asked if he had yet discovered any traces of the person to whom it was addressed. The messenger laid the letter down so close to Darnay that he saw the direction--the more quickly because it was his own right name. The address, turned into English, ran:

> "Very pressing. To Monsieur heretofore
> the Marquis St. Evremonde, of France.

Confided to the cares of Messrs. Tellson and

Co., Bankers, London, England."

On the marriage morning, Doctor Manette had made it

his one urgent and express request to Charles Darnay

that the secret of this name should be--unless he, the

Doctor, dissolved the obligation--kept inviolate between

them. Nobody else knew it to be his name. His own wife

had no suspicion of the fact. Mr. Lorry could have

none.

"No," said Mr. Lorry, in reply to the messenger. "I

have referred it, I think, to everybody now here, and no

one can tell me where this gentleman is to be found."

Darnay, unable to restrain himself any longer, said,

"I know the fellow."

"Will you take charge of the letter?" said Mr.

Lorry. "Do you know where to deliver it?"

"I do."

"Will you undertake to explain that we suppose it to

have been addressed here on the chance of our knowing

where to forward it and that it has been here some

time?"

"I will do so. Do you start for Paris from here?"

"From here, at eight."

"I will come back, to see you off."

Very ill at ease with himself, Darnay made the best of his way into the quiet of the Temple, opened the letter, and read it. These were its contents:

"Prison of the Abbeye, Paris.

June 21, 1792.

"Monsieur heretofore the Marquis,

"After having long been in danger of my life, at the hands of the village, I have been seized, with great violence and indignity.

"The crime for which I am imprisoned, Monsieur heretofore the Marquis, and for which I shall be summoned before the tribunal, and shall lose my life (without your so generous help) is, they tell me, treason against the majesty of the people in that I have acted against them for an emigrant.

"Ah! most gracious Monsieur heretofore the Marquis, where is that emigrant? I cry in my sleep, 'where is he?' I demand of Heaven, will he not come to deliver me? No answer. Monsieur heretofore the Marquis, I send my desolate cry across the sea, hoping it may perhaps reach your ears through the great bank of Tellson, known at Paris!

"For the love of Heaven, of justice, of generosity, of the honor of your noble name, I supplicate you, Monsieur heretofore the Marquis, to succor and release me.

Your afflicted,

Gabelle"

The latent uneasiness in Darnay's mind was roused to vigorous life by this letter. The peril of an old servant and a good one, whose only crime was fidelity to himself and his family, stared him so reproachfully in the face that, as he walked to and fro in the Temple considering what to do, he almost hid his face from the passers-by.

Monsieur Gabelle had held the impoverished and involved estate, on written instructions, to spare the people, to give them what little there was to give--such fuel as the heavy creditors would let them have in the winter, and such produce as could be saved from the same grip in the summer--and no doubt he had put the fact, in plea and proof for his own safety, so that it could not but appear now.

This favored the desperate resolution Charles Darnay had begun to make, that he would go to Paris.

That night--it was the fourteenth of August--he sat up late, and wrote two fervent letters. One was to Lucie, explaining the strong obligation he was under to go to Paris, and showing her at length the reasons that he had for feeling confident that he would become involved in no personal danger there. The other was to the Doctor, confiding Lucie and their dear child to his care and dwelling on the same topics with the strongest assurances. To both he wrote that he would dispatch letters in proof of his safety immediately after his arrival.

The unseen force was drawing him fast to itself now, and all the tides and winds were setting straight and strong towards it. He left his two letters with a trusty porter to be delivered half an hour before midnight, and no sooner, took horse for Dover, and began his journey. "For the love of Heaven, of justice, of generosity, of the honor of your noble name!" was the poor prisoner's cry, with which he strengthened his sinking heart, as he left all that was dear on earth behind him.

The traveler fared slowly on his way, who fared towards Paris from England in the autumn of the year one thousand seven hundred and ninety-two. More than enough of bad roads, bad equipages, and bad horses he would have encountered to delay him, though the fallen and unfortunate King of France had been upon his throne in all his glory; but, the changed times were fraught with other obstacles than these. Every town-gate and village taxing-house had its own band of citizen-patriots, with their national muskets in a most explosive state of readiness, who stopped all comers and goers, cross-questioned them, inspected their papers, looked for their names in lists of their own, turned them back, or sent them on, or stopped them and laid them in hold, as their capricious judgment or fancy deemed best, for the dawning Republic one and indivisible, of liberty, equality, fraternity, or death.

A very few French leagues of his journey were accomplished when Charles Darnay began to perceive that, whatever might befall now, he must on to his journey's end. Not a mean village closed upon him, not a common barrier dropped across the road behind him, but he knew it to be another iron door in the series that was barred between him and England. The universal watchfulness so encompassed him, that if he had been taken in a net or were being forwarded to his destination in a cage, he could not have felt his freedom more completely gone.

Nothing but the production of the afflicted Gabelle's letter from his prison of the Abbeye would have got him on so far. His difficulty at the guard house in this small place had been such that he felt his journey to have come to a crisis, and he was therefore as little surprised as a man could be to find himself awakened at the small inn to which he had been admitted until morning in the middle of the night.

Awakened by a timid, local functionary and three armed patriots in rough red caps and with pipes in their mouths, who sat down on the bed. "Emigrant," said the functionary, "I am going to send you on to Paris under an escort."

"Citizen," replied Darnay, "I desire nothing more than to get to Paris, though I could dispense with the escort."

"Silence!" growled a red cap, striking at the coverlet with the butt-end of his musket. "Peace, aristocrat."

"It is as the good patriot says," observed the timid functionary. "You are an aristocrat and must have an escort and must pay for it."

"I have no choice," said Charles Darnay.

"Choice, listen to him," said the scowling redcap. "As if it was not a favor to be protected from the lamp iron."

"It is always as the good patriot says," observed the functionary. "Rise and dress yourself, emigrant."

Darnay complied and was taken back to the guardhouse where other patriots in rough red caps were smoking, drinking, and sleeping by a watch fire. Here, he paid a heavy price for his escort. And hence he started with it on the wet, wet roads, at three o'clock in the morning. They traveled a day and a night, before daylight at last found them before the wall of Paris.

The barrier was closed and strongly guarded when they rode up to it.

"Where are the papers of this prisoner?" demanded a resolute-looking man in authority who was summoned out by the guard.

A numerous medley of men and women, not to mention beasts and vehicles of various sorts, was waiting to issue forth. But, the previous identification was so strict that they filtered through the barrier very slowly. When he had sat in his saddle some half hour, Darnay found himself confronted by the same man in authority who directed the guard to open the barrier. Then he delivered to the escort, drunk and sober, a receipt for the escorted, and requested him to dismount. He did so, and the two patriots, leading his tired horse, turned and rode away without entering the city.

He accompanied his conductor into a guard-room, smelling of common wine and tobacco where certain soldiers and patriots, asleep and awake, drunk and sober, were standing and lying about. Some registers were lying open on a desk, and an officer of a coarse, dark aspect, presided over these.

"Citizen Defarge," said he to Darnay's conductor, as he took a slip of paper to write on. "Is this the emigrant, Evremonde? The Marquis Saint Evremonde?"

"This is our man!"

"You are consigned, Evremonde, to the prison of La Force."

"Just Heaven!" exclaimed Darnay. "Under what law? And, for what offense?"

The officer looked up from his slip of paper for a moment, "We have new laws, Evremonde, and new offenses, since you were here." He said it with a hard smile. Defarge motioned to the prisoner that he must accompany him. The prisoner obeyed, and a guard of two armed patriots attended them.

"Is it you," said Defarge in a low voice as he went down the guarded steps and turned into Paris, "who married the daughter of Doctor Manette, once a prisoner in the Bastille, that is no more?"

"Yes," replied Darnay, looking at him with surprise.

"My name is Defarge, and I keep a wine shop in the Quartier Saint Antoine. Possibly, you have heard of me?"

"My 'wife' came to your house to reclaim her father. Yes."

The word wife seemed to serve as a gloomy reminder to Defarge to say with sudden impatience, "In the name of that sharp female, newly born, and called La Guillotine, why did you come to France?"

"In answer to the appeal of a fellow country-man. Do you not believe it is the truth?"

Defarge glanced darkly at him for answer, and walked on in a steady, set silence. The deeper he sank into this silence, the fainter hope there was, or so Darnay thought, of his softening in any slight degree. He therefore made haste to say, "It is of the utmost importance to me, (you know citizen, even better than I, of how much importance), that I should be able to communicate to Mr. Lorry, of Tellson's Bank, an English gentleman who is now in Paris, the simple fact, without comment, that I have been thrown into the prison of La Force. Will you cause this to be done for me?"

"I will do," Defarge doggedly rejoined, "nothing for you. My duty is to my country and the people. I am the sworn servant of both against you. I will do nothing for you."

The prison of La Force was a gloomy prison, dark and filthy, with a horrible smell of foul sleep in it. Extraordinary how soon the noise and flavor of imprisoned sleep becomes manifest in all such places that are ill-cared for. Through the dismal prison twilight, Darnay was taken by corridor and staircase, many doors clanging and locking behind them, until they came into a large, low, vaulted chamber, crowded with prisoners of both sexes.

There was a murmur of commiseration as Charles Darnay crossed the room to a grated door where the jailer awaited him. And many voices, among which the soft and compassionate voices of women were conspicuous, gave him good wishes and encouragement. He turned at the grated door to render thanks of his heart. It closed under the jailer's hand, and the apparitions vanished from his sight, forever.

Tellson's Bank, established in the Saint Germain quarter of Paris, was in a wing of a large house, approached by a courtyard, and shut off from the street by a high wall, under strong gate. Mr. Jarvis Lorry, sat by a newly lighted wood fire and on his honest and courageous face there was a deeper shade than the pendant lamp could throw, or any object in the room distortedly reflect. A shade, of horror. From the streets beyond the high wall and the strong gate, there came the usual night-hum of the city, with now and then an indescribable ring in it--weird, and unearthly, as if some unwanted sounds of a terrible nature were going up to heaven. "Thank God," said Mr. Lorry, clasping his hands, "that no one near and dear to me is in this dreadful town tonight. May He have mercy on all who are in danger.

Soon afterwards, the bell at the great gate sounded. But, there was no loud eruption into the courtyard as he had expected, and he heard the gate clash again, and all was quiet--until, his door suddenly opened and two figures rushed in, at sight of which, he fell back in amazement--Lucie and her father.

"What is this?" cried Mr. Lorry, breathless and confused. "What is the matter, Lucie, Manette? What has happened? What has brought you here? What is it?"

With a look, fixed upon him in her paleness and wildness, she panted out in his arms, imploringly, "Oh! my dear friend, my husband!"

"Your husband, Lucie?"

"Charles."

"What of Charles?"

"Here."

"Here? In Paris?"

"He has been here some days, three or four. I don't know how many. I can't collect my thoughts. An errand of generosity brought him here, unknown to us. He was stopped at the barrier and sent to prison."

The old man uttered an irrepressible cry. Almost at the same moment, the bell of the great gate rang again, and a loud noise of feet and voices came pouring into the courtyard.

"What is that noise?" said the doctor, turning towards the window.

"Oh! don't look!" cried Mr. Lorry. "Don't look out, Manette, for your life, don't touch the blind."

The Doctor turned, with his hand upon the fastening of the window and said with a cool, bold smile, "My dear friend, I have a charmed life in this city. I have been a Bastille prisoner. There is no patriot in Paris--in Paris, in France--who, knowing me to have been a prisoner in the Bastille, would touch me--except to overwhelm me with embraces or carry me in triumph. My old pain has given me a power that has brought us through the barrier and gained us news of Charles and brought us here."

He looked out upon a throng of men and women, not

enough in number or near enough to fill the courtyard--
not more than forty or fifty in all. The people in
possession of the house had let them in at the gate and
they had rushed in to work at the grindstone. It had
evidently been set up there for their purpose as in a
convenient and retired spot--but, such awful workers,
and such awful work. The grindstone had a double
handle, and turning at it madly were two men whose faces
--as their long hair flapped back when the whirlings of
the grindstone brought their faces up--were more
horrible and cruel than the visages of the wildest
savages in their most barbarous disguise. False eyebrows and false mustaches were stuck upon them. And
their hideous countenances were all bloody and sweaty
and all awry with howling and all staring and glaring
with beastly excitement and want of sleep.

"They are," Mr. Lorry whispered the words, glancing
fearfully round at the locked room, "murdering the
prisoners. If you are sure of what you say, if you
really have the power you think you have, as I believe

you have, make yourself known to those devils and get taken to La Force. It may be too late, I don't know, but, let it not be a minute later."

Doctor Manette pressed his hand, hastened bareheaded out of the room, and was in the courtyard when Mr. Lorry regained the blind. His streaming white hair, his remarkable face, and the impetuous confidence of his manner, as he put the weapons aside like water, carried him in an instant to the heart of the concourse at the stone. For a few moments there was a pause, and a hurry, and a murmur, and the unintelligible sound of his voice. And then Mr. Lorry saw him, surrounded by all, and in the midst of a line of twenty men long, all linked shoulder-to-shoulder and hand-to-shoulder, hurried out with the cries of "Live the Bastille prisoner. Help for the Bastille prisoner's kindred in La Force. Room for the Bastille prisoner in front there. Save the prisoner Evremonde at La Force," and a thousand answering shouts.

He closed the lattice again with a fluttering heart;

closed the window and the curtain, hastened to Lucie, and told her that her father was assisted by the people, and gone in search of her husband.

He found her child and Miss Pross with her. But, it never occurred to him to be surprised by their appearance until a long time afterwards when he sat watching them in such quiet as the night knew.

Doctor Manette did not return until the morning of the fourth day of his absence. So much of what had happened in that dreadful time as could be kept from the knowledge of Lucie was so well concealed from her that not until long afterwards, when France and she were far apart, did she know that eleven hundred defenseless prisoners of both sexes and all ages had been killed by the populace. That four days and nights had been darkened by this deed of horror. And, that the air around her had been tainted by the slain.

The Doctor had tried hard and never ceased trying to get Charles Darnay set at liberty--or at least to get him brought to trial. But, the public current of the time set too strong and fast for him. The new era began, the King was tried, doomed, and beheaded. The Republic of liberty, equality, fraternity or death declared for victory or death against the world in arms. The black flag waved night and day from the great towers of Notre-Dame.

One year and three months passed, and during all that time Lucie was never sure from hour to hour but that the guillotine would strike off her husband's head next day. Every day, through the stony streets, the tumbrels now jolted heavily, filled with condemned. Lovely girls; bright women, brown haired, black haired and gray; youths, stalwart men, and old; gentle-born and peasant-born; all red wine for La Guillotine; all daily brought into the light from the dark cellars of the loathsome prison, and carried to her through the street to slake her devouring thirst.

Then, on a December day, her father imparted, to Lucie, the news: Charles is summoned for tomorrow.

"For tomorrow?"

"There is no time to lose! I am well prepared, but there are precautions to be taken that could not be taken until he was actually summoned before the tribunal. He has not received the notice yet, but, I know that he will be presently summoned for tomorrow and removed to the Conciergerie. I have timely information. You are not afraid?"

She could scarcely answer, "I trust in you."

"Do so, implicitly. Your suspense is nearly ended, my darling. He shall be restored to you within a few hours. I have encompassed him with every protection."

The dread tribunal of five judges, public prosecutor, and determined jury, sat every day. Their lists went forth every evening and were read out by the jailers of the various prisons to their prisoners. The standard jailer joke was, "Come out and listen to the evening paper, you inside there!"

Charles Evremonde, called Darnay, was at length arraigned. His judges sat upon the bench in feathered hats. But, the rough red cap and tri-colored cockade was the headdress otherwise prevailing.

Looking at the jury and the turbulent audience, he might have thought that the usual order of things was reversed and that the felons were trying the honest men. Charles Evremonde, called Darnay, was accused by the public prosecutor as an emigrant, whose life was forfeit to the Republic under the decree which banished all emigrants on pain of death. It was nothing that the decree bore date since his return to France. There he was, and there was the decree. He had been taken in France and his head was demanded.

"Take off his head," cried the audience. "An enemy to the Republic."

The president rang his bell to silence those cries and ask the prisoner whether it was not true that he had lived many years in England.

Undoubtedly, it was.

Was he not an emigrant, then? What did he call himself?

Not an emigrant, he hoped within the sense and

spirit of the law.

Why not? the president desired to know.

Because he had voluntarily relinquished a title that was distasteful to him.

What proof had he of this?

He handed him the names of two witnesses: Dalefield Gabelle and Alexandre Manette.

But he had married in England, the president reminded him.

True, but not an English woman.

A citizeness of France?

Yes, by birth.

Her name and family?

"Lucie Manette, only daughter of Doctor Manette, the good physician, who sits there."

This answer had a happy effect upon the audience. Cries in exaltation of the well-known, good physician rent the hall.

(End of Side 3)

On these few steps of his dangerous way, Charles Darnay had set his foot according to Doctor Manette's reiterated instructions. The same cautious counsel directed every step that lay before him and had prepared every inch of his road. At last, the jury declared that they had heard enough, that they were ready with their votes if the president were content to receive them. At every vote the jurymen voted aloud and individually. The populace set up a shout of applause, all the voices were in the prisoner's favor, and the president declared him free.

After grasping the Doctor's hand as he stood victorious and proud before him; after grasping the hand of Mr. Lorry; after kissing little Lucie, who was lifted up to clasp her arms round his neck; and after embracing the ever zealous and faithful Pross, who lifted her; Darnay took his wife in his arms.

"Lucie, my own, I'm safe!"

"Oh dearest Charles, let me thank God for this on my knees, as I have prayed to him."

They all reverently bowed their heads and hearts.

When she was again in his arms, he said to her, "I now speak to your father, dearest. No other man, in all this France, could have done what he has done for me."

She laid her head upon her father's breast, as she had laid his poor head upon her own breast, long, long ago.

He was happy in the return he had made her. He was recompensed for his suffering. He was proud of his strength. "You must not be weak, my darling." he remonstrated. "Don't tremble so. I have saved him."

"I have saved him." It was not another of the dreams in which he had often come back. He was really here. And yet, his wife trembled, and a vague but heavy fear was upon her. All the air around, was so thick and dark. The people were so passionately revengeful and fitful, the innocent were so constantly put to death on vague suspicion and black malice. It was so impossible to forget that many, as blameless as her husband, and as dear to others as he was to her, every day shared the fate from which he had been clutched, that her heart could not be as lightened of its load as she felt it ought to be.

The shadows of a wintry afternoon, were beginning to fall, and even now the dreadful carts were rolling through the streets. Her mind pursued them, looking for him among the condemned. And then, she clung closer to his real presence and trembled more. Her father, cheering her, showed a compassionate superiority to this woman's weaknesses, which was wonderful to see. No garret, no shoemaking, no One Hundred and Five, North Tower, now. He had accomplished the task he had set himself. His promise was redeemed. He had saved Charles. Let them all lean upon him.

The housekeeping was of a very frugal kind. Not only because that was the safest way of life, involving the least offense to the people, but because they were not rich. Charles, throughout his imprisonment had had to pay heavily for his bad food and for his guard, and towards the living of the poorer prisoners. Partly on this account, and partly to avoid a domestic spy, they kept no servant. The citizen and citizeness who acted as porters at the courtyard gate rendered them occasional service; and Jerry, almost wholly transferred to them by Mr. Lorry, had become their daily retainer, and had his bed there every night.

For some months past, Miss Pross and Jerry Cruncher had discharged the office of purveyors--the former carrying the money, the latter the basket. Every afternoon, at about the time when the public lamps were lighted, they fared forth on this duty and made and brought home such purchases as were needful.

"Now, Mr. Cruncher," said Miss Pross, whose eyes were red with felicity, "if you are ready, I am."

Jerry hoarsely professed himself at Miss Pross' service.

"Pray, pray be cautious," cried Lucie.

"Yes, yes, yes, I'll be cautious," said Miss Pross, "but, may I ask a question, Doctor Manette, before I go?"

"I think you might take that liberty," the doctor answered smiling.

"Is there," asked the good woman, "any prospect yet, of our getting out of this place?"

"I fear not yet. It would be dangerous for Charles yet."

"Heigh, ho-hum," said Miss Pross, cheerfully repressing a sigh, as she glanced at her darling's golden hair in the light of the fire, "then we must have patience and wait: that's all."

They went out, leaving Lucie and her husband, her father, and the child, by a bright fire. All was subdued and quiet. And Lucie was more at ease than she had been.

"What is that?" she cried all at once.

"My dear," said her father, stopping in his story and laying his hand on hers, "command yourself. What a disordered state you are in. The least thing, nothing, startles you. You, your father's daughter."

"I thought, my father," said Lucie, excusing herself

with a pale face, and in a faltering voice, "that I heard strange feet upon the stairs."

"My love, the staircase is as still as death." As he said the word, a blow was struck upon the door.

"Oh! father, father, what can this be? Hide Charles. Save him!"

"My child," said the doctor, rising and laying his hand upon her shoulder, "I have saved him. What weakness is this, my dear! Let me go to the door." He took the lamp in his hand, crossed the two intervening outer rooms and opened it. A rude clattering of feet over the floor, and four rough men in red caps, armed with sabers and pistols entered the room.

"The citizen, Evremonde, called Darnay," said the first.

"Who seeks him?" answered Darnay.

"I seek him. We seek him. I know you, Evremonde. I saw you before the tribunal. You are again the prisoner of the Republic."

The four surrounded him where he stood with his wife

and child clinging to him.

"Tell me, how and why, am I again a prisoner."

"It is enough that you return straight to the Conciergerie and will know tomorrow. You are summoned for tomorrow."

Happily unconscious of the new calamity at home, Miss Pross threaded her way along the narrow streets and crossed the river by the bridge of the Pont Neuf, reckoning, in her mind the number of indispensable purchases she had to make. Jerry, with the basket walked at her side. Having purchased a few small articles of grocery and a measure of oil for the lamp, Miss Pross bethought herself of the wine they wanted. After peeping into several wine shops she stopped at the sign of the Good Republican Brutus of Antiquity, not far from the National Palace.

As their wine was measuring out, a man parted from another man in a corner and rose to depart. In going, he had to face Miss Pross. No sooner did he face her, than Miss Pross uttered a scream, and clapped her hands.

"What is the matter?" said the man, who had caused Miss Pross to scream, speaking in a vexed, abrupt voice, though in a low tone and in English.

"Oh, oh, Solomon, dear Solomon," cried Miss Pross, clapping her hands again. "After not setting eyes upon you, or hearing of you for so long a time, do I find you, here?"

"Don't call me Solomon. Do you want to be the death of me?" asked the man in a furtive, frightened way.

"Oh! brother, brother," cried Miss Pross, bursting into tears. "Have I ever been so hard with you that you ask me such a cruel question?"

"Then hold your meddlesome tongue," said Solomon, "and come out if you want to speak to me. Pay for your wine and come out! Who is this man?"

Miss Pross, shaking her loving and dejected head at her, by no means, affectionate brother, said through her tears, "Mr. Cruncher."

"Then let him come out, too," said Solomon. "Does he think me a ghost?"

Apparently, Mr. Cruncher did, to judge from his looks. He said not a word, however, and Miss Pross, exploring the depths of her reticule, through her tears, with great difficulty, paid for her wine.

"If you expected me to be surprised," said her brother Solomon, at the dark street corner, "I am not surprised. I knew you were here. I know of most people who are here. If you really don't want to endanger my existence, which I half believe you do, go your ways as soon as possible and let me go mine. I am busy, I am an official."

Mr. Cruncher then touched him on the shoulder and hoarsely and unexpectedly interposed with the following, singular question. "I say, might I ask a favor? As to whether your name is John Solomon or Solomon John?"

The official turned towards him with sudden distrust. He had not previously uttered a word.

"Come," said Mr. Cruncher, "Speak out, you know. John Solomon or Solomon John? "She calls you Solomon, and she must know, being your sister, and I know you're

John, you know. Now which of the two comes first, eh? And, regarding that name of Pross, likewise. That weren't your name over the water. I swear it was a name of two syllables."

"Indeed."

"Yes, t'other one was one syllable. I know you. You was a spy witness at the Bailey. What, in the name of the Father of Lies, own father to yourself, was you called at that time?"

"Barsad," said another voice, striking in.

"Ah, that's the name for a thousand pounds," cried Jerry.

The speaker who struck in was Sydney Carton. He had his hands behind him under the skirts of his riding coat, and he stood at Mr. Cruncher's elbow as negligently as he might have stood at the Old Bailey itself.

"Oh, don't be alarmed, my dear Miss Pross," he continued. "I arrived at Mr. Lorry's, to his surprise, yesterday evening. We agreed that I would not present myself elsewhere until all was well--or, unless I could be useful. I present myself here to beg a little talk with your brother. I wish you had a better employed brother, than Mr. Barsad. I wish, for your sake, Mr. Barsad was not a sheep of the prisons."

Sheep was a cant word of the time, for spy, under the jailers. The spy, who was pale, turned paler, and asked him how he dared.

"I'll tell you," said Sydney, "I lighted on you, Mr. Barsad, coming out of the prison of the Conciergerie, while I was contemplating the walls, an hour or more ago. You have a face to be remembered, and I remember faces well. Could you favor me, in confidence, with some minutes of your company, at the office of Tellson's Bank, for instance?"

"Under a threat?"

"Oh, did I say that?"

"Then why should I go there?"

"Really, Mr. Barsad, I can't say, if you can't."

"Do you mean that you won't say, sir?" the spy

irresolutely asked.

"You apprehend me, very clearly, Mr. Barsad, I won't."

"I'll hear what you've got to say. Yes, I'll go with you."

Mr. Lorry had just finished his dinner, and was sitting before a cheery little log or two of fire. He turned his head as they entered and showed the surprise with which he saw a stranger.

"Miss Pross's brother, sir," said Sydney. Mr. Barsad."

"Barsad," repeated the old gentleman, "Barsad, I have an association with the name and with the face."

"I told you you had a remarkable face, Mr. Barsad," observed Carton, coolly. "Pray, sit down."

As he took a chair himself, he supplied the link that Mr. Lorry wanted, by saying to him with a frown, "Witness at Darnay's trial at the Old Bailey."

Mr. Lorry immediately remembered and regarded his new visitor with an undisguised look of abhorrence.

"Mr. Barsad has been recognized by Miss Pross as her affectionate brother," said Sydney, "and has acknowledged the relationship. I pass to worse news. Darnay has been arrested again."

Struck with consternation the old gentleman exclaimed, "What do you tell me? I left him safe and free within these two hours and am about to return to him."

"Arrested for all that. When was it done, Mr. Barsad?"

"Just now, if at all."

"Mr. Barsad is the best authority possible, sir," said Sydney, "and I have it from Mr. Barsad's communication to a friend and brother sheep over a bottle of wine that the arrest has taken place. Now," said Sydney, "this is a desperate time, when desperate games are played for desperate stakes. No man's life here is worth purchase. Anyone carried home by the people today may be condemned tomorrow. And the stake I have resolved to play for, in case of the worst, is a friend in the Conciergerie. And the friend I purpose to myself to win is Mr. Barsad."

"You need have good cards, sir," said the spy.

"I'll run them over and see what I hold. Mr. Barsad," he went on, in the tone of one who really was looking over hand of cards: "Sheep of the prisons, emissary of republican committees, now turnkey, now prisoner, always spy and secret informer, so much the more valuable here for being English that an Englishman is less open to suspicion of subornation in those characters than a Frenchman, represents himself to his employers under a false name. Ha! Ha! That's a very good card. Mr. Barsad, now in the employ of the republican French government, was formerly in the employ of the aristocratic English government--the enemy of France and freedom. Inference clear as a day in this region of suspicion, that Mr. Barsad, still in the pay of the aristocratic English government, is the spy of Pitt. Ha! Ha! The treacherous flow of the Republic, crouching in its bosom, the English traitor and agent of all mischief so much spoken of, and so difficult to find. That's a card not to be beaten. Have you followed my hand, Mr. Barsad?"

With a countenance decidedly paler than before, the sheep of the prisons turned to Sydney Carton and said, "It has come to a point. I go on duty soon, and can't overstay my time. You told me you had a proposal. What is it?"

"Not very much. You are a turnkey, at the Conciergerie?"

"I tell you, once and for all, there is no such thing as an escape possible," said the spy firmly.

"Why need you tell me what I have not asked? You are a turnkey at the Conciergerie?"

"I am, sometimes."

"You can be, when you choose."

"I can pass in and out when I choose."

Sydney Carton, filled a glass with brandy, poured it slowly out upon the hearth, and watched it as it dropped. It being all spent, he said, rising, "Come into the dark-room here, and let us have one final word, alone."

It was ten o'clock at night, when Sydney Carton, stood before the prison of La Force. He stood in the middle of the street under a glimmering lamp, and wrote with his pencil on a scrap of paper. Then, traversing with a decided step of one who remembered the way well, several dark and dirty streets--much dirtier than usual for the best public thoroughfares remained uncleansed in those times of terror,- he stopped at a chemist shop, which the owner was closing with his own hands. A small, dim, crooked shop, kept in a tortuous uphill thoroughfare, by a small dim, crooked man. Giving this citizen "good-night" as he confronted him at his counter --he laid the scrap of paper before him.

"Whoo," the chemist whistled softly as he read it. Sydney Carton took no heed, and the chemist said, "For you, citizen?"

"For me."

"You will be careful to keep them separate, citizen?

You know the consequences of mixing them?"

"Perfectly."

Certain, small packets were made and given to him. He put them, one by one, in the breast of his inner coat, counted out the money for them, and deliberately left the shop.

"There is nothing more to do," said he, glancing upwards at the moon, "until tomorrow. I can't sleep." The night wore out, and as he stood upon the bridge listening to the water as it splashed the river walls of the island of Paris, where the picturesque confusion of houses and cathedral shone bright in the light of the moon, the day came coldly, looking like a dead face out of the sky. Then the night, with the moon and the stars, turned pale, and died. And for a little while, it seemed as if creation were delivered over to Death's dominion. But, the glorious sun, rising, seemed to strike those words, that burden of the night, straight and warm to his heart, in its long, bright rays, and looking long them with reverently shaded eyes, a bridge of light appeared to span the air between him and the sun while the river sparkled under it.

Mr. Lorry was already out when he got back, and it was easy to surmise where the good old man was gone. Sydney Carton drank nothing but a little coffee, ate some bread, and having washed and changed to refresh himself, went out to the place of trial.

The court was all astir and abuzz when the black sheep--who many fell away from in dread--pressed him into an obscure corner among the crowd. Mr. Lorry was there and Doctor Manette was there. She was there, sitting beside her father.

When her husband was brought in, she turned a look upon him so sustaining, so encouraging, so full of admiring love and pitying tenderness--yet, so courageous, for his sake, that it called the healthy blood into his face, brightened his glance and animated his heart. If there had been any eyes to notice the influence of her look on Sydney Carton, it would have been seen to be the same influence exactly.

Before that unjust tribunal there was little or no order of procedure insuring to any accused person any reasonable hearing. There could have been no such revolution if all law, forms and ceremonies, had not first been so monstrously abused that the suicidal vengeance of the Revolution was to scatter them all to the winds.

Every eye turned to the five judges and the public prosecutor--no favorable leaning in that quarter today. A fell, uncompromising, murderous, business meaning there. Every eye then sought some other eye in the crowd, and gleamed at it approvingly, and heads nodded at one another before bending forward with a strained attention.

"Charles Evremonde, called Darnay. Released yesterday. Re-accused and re-taken yesterday. Indictment delivered to him last night. Suspected and denounced enemy of the Republic, aristocrat, one of a family of tyrants, one of a race proscribed for that they had used their abolished privileges to the infamous oppression of the people. Charles Evremonde, called Darnay, in right of such proscription, absolutely dead in law."

At every juryman's vote there was a roar, another and another, roar and roar. Unanimously voted. At heart and by dissent an aristocrat, an enemy of the Republic, a notorious oppressor of the People. Back to the Conciergerie and Death within twenty-four hours.

The wretched wife of the innocent man thus doomed to die fell under the sentence as if she had been mortally stricken. But she uttered no sound, so strong was the voice within her, representing that it was she, of all the world who must uphold him in his misery and not augment it, that it quickly raised her, even from that shock.

The judges having to take part in a public demonstration out of doors, the tribunal adjourned. The quick noise and movement of the court's emptying itself by many passages had not ceased when Lucie stood stretching out her arms towards her husband, with nothing in her face but love and consolation.

"If I might touch him! If I might embrace him once. Oh! good citizens, if you would have so much compassion for us."

There was but a jailer left, along with two of the four men who had taken him last night, and Barsad. The people had all poured out to the show in the streets. Barsad proposed to the rest, "Let her embrace him then. It is but a moment." It was silently acquiesced in, they passed her over the seats in the hall to a raised place where he, by leaning over the dock, could hold her in his arms. As he was drawn away, his wife released him and stood looking after him with her hands touching one another in the attitude of prayer and with a radiant look upon her face in which there was even a comforting smile. As he went out at the prisoner's door she turned, laid her head lovingly on her father's breast, tried to speak to him and fell at his feet.

Then, issuing from the obscure corner, from which he had never moved, Sydney Carton came and took her up.

Only her father and Mr. Lorry were with her. His arm trembled, as it raised her, and supported her head. Yet, there was an air about him, that was not all of pity--that had a flush of pride in it.

"Shall I take her to a coach? I shall never feel her weight." He carried her lightly to the door and laid her tenderly down in a coach. Her father and her old friend got into it, and he took his seat beside the driver.

"Before I go," Carton said, and paused, "I may kiss her?"

It was remembered afterwards that when he bent down, and touched her face with his lips, he murmured some words. The child, who was nearest to him, told them afterwards, and told her grandchildren, when she was a handsome old lady, that she heard him say, "A life you love."

In the black prison of the Conciergerie, the doomed of the day awaited their fate. They were in number as the weeks of the year. Fifty-two were to roll that afternoon, on the life-tide of the city to the boundless everlasting sea. Before their souls were quit of them, new occupants were appointed. Before their blood ran into the blood spilled yesterday, the blood that was to mingle with theirs tomorrow was already set apart.

Charles Darnay, alone in a cell, had sustained himself with no flattering delusions since he came to it from the tribunal. In every line of the narrative he had heard, he had heard his condemnation. When he lay down on his straw bed, he thought he had done with this world. But it beckoned him back in his sleep and showed itself in shining forms. Free and happy, back in the old house in Soho, (though it had nothing in it like the real house), unaccountably released and light of heart, he was with Lucie again, and she told him it was all a dream, and he had never gone away. A pause of forgetfulness, and then, he had even suffered and had come back to her, dead and at peace, and yet there was no difference in him. Another pause of oblivion and then he awoke in the somber morning, unconscious where he was or what had happened. Until, it flashed upon his mind, "this is the day of my death."

The hours went on, and the clock struck the numbers he would never hear again: nine--gone forever; ten--gone forever; eleven--gone forever; twelve--coming on to pass away.

Walking regularly to and fro with his arms folded on his breast, he heard one struck away from him without surprise. The hour had measured like most other hours. Devoutly thankful to heaven for his recovered self-possession, he thought, "There is but another now," and turned to walk again.

Footsteps in the stone passage, outside the door. He stopped. The door was quickly opened and closed. And there, stood before him, face-to-face, quiet, intent upon him, with the light of a smile on his features, and a cautionary finger on his lip, Sydney Carton.

"Of all the people upon earth, you least expected to see me," he said.

"I could not believe it to be you. I can scarcely

believe it, now. You are not," apprehension came suddenly into his mind, "a prisoner?"

"No! I am accidentally possessed of a power over one of the keepers here. And, in virtue of it, I stand before you. I come here from her, your wife, dear Darnay."

The prisoner wrung his hands.

"I bring you a request from her."

"What is it?"

"A most earnest, pressing and emphatic entreaty, addressed to you in the most pathetic tones of the voice so dear to you that you well remember." The prisoner turned his face, partly aside, "You have no time to ask me why I bring it, or what it means. I have no time to tell you. You must comply with it. Now take off those boots you wear and draw on these of mine."

"Carton, there is no escaping from this place. It can never be done. You will only die with me. It is madness!"

"It would be madness if I asked you to escape. But,

do I? When I ask you to pass out of that door, tell me it is madness and remain here. Now, change that cravat for this one of mine, that coat for this of mine, while you do it, let me take this ribbon from your hair. Shake out your hair like this of mine."

With wonderful quickness, and with a strength both of will and action that appeared quite supernatural, he forced all these changes upon him. The prisoner was like a young child in his hands.

"There are a pen, and ink, and paper, on this table," continued Carton. "Is your hand steady enough to write?"

"It was, when you came in."

"Well, steady it again, and write what I shall dictate. Quick friend, quick."

Pressing his hand to his bewildered head, Darnay sat down at the table. Carton, with his right hand in his breast, stood close beside him.

"Write exactly as I speak."

"To whom do I address it?"

"To no one." Carton still had his hand in his breast.

"Do I date it?"

"No!"

The prisoner looked up at each question, Carton standing over him with his hand in his breast looking down.

"If you remember," said Carton, dictating, "the words that passed between us long ago, you will readily comprehend this when you see it. You do remember them, I know. It is not in your nature to forget them." He was drawing his hand from his breast. The prisoner chancing to look up in his hurried wonder as he wrote, the hand stopped, closing upon something. "Have you written, 'forget them?'" Carton asked.

"I have. Is that a weapon in your hand?"

"No, I am not armed."

"What is it in your hand?"

"You shall know directly. Write on! There are but a few words more." He dictated again. "I am thankful that the time has come when I can prove them. That I do so, is no subject for regret, or grief." As he said these words, with his eyes fixed on the writer, his hand slowly and softly, moved down close to the writer's face. The pen dropped from Darnay's fingers on the table, and he looked about him vacantly.

"What vapor is that?" he asked.

"Vapor?"

"Something that crossed me."

"I am conscious of nothing. There can be nothing here. Take up the pen and finish, hurry, hurry!" As if his memory were impaired, or his faculties disordered, the prisoner made an effort to rally his attention. As he looked at Carton, with clouded eyes, and with an altered manner of breathing, Carton, his hand again in his breast, looked steadily at him:

"Hurry! Hurry!" The prisoner bent over the paper once more, "If it had been otherwise," Carton's hand was again watchfully and softly stealing down, "I never should have used the longer opportunity. If it had been otherwise," the hand was at the prisoner's face, "I should but have had so much the more to answer for. If it had been otherwise," Carton looked at the pen and saw it was trailing off into unintelligible signs. Carton's hand moved back to his breast no more. The prisoner sprang up with a reproachful look, but Carton's hand was close and firm at his nostrils, and Carton's left arm caught him round the waist.

For a few seconds, Darnay faintly struggled with the man who had come to lay down his life for him. But within a minute or so, he was stretched insensible on the ground. Quickly, but with hands as true to the purpose as his heart was, Carton dressed himself in the clothes the prisoner had laid aside, combed back his hair, and tied it with the ribbon the prisoner had worn. Then, he softly called, "Enter there! Come in!" and the spy presented himself.

"You see," said Carton, looking up, as he kneeled on one knee beside the insensible figure, putting the paper in the breast. "Is your hazard very great?"

"Now, get assistance, and take me to the coach."

"You?" said the spy, nervously.

"Him, man! With whom I have exchanged. You go out at the gate by which you brought me in."

"Of course."

"I was weak and faint when you brought me in, and I am fainter now you take me out. The parting interview has overpowered me. Such things happen here often, too often. Your life is in your own hands. Now, quick! Call assistance!"

"You swear not to betray me," said the trembling spy as he paused for a last moment.

"Don't fear me, I will be true to the death."

The door closed and Sydney Carton was left alone. Straining his powers of listening to the utmost, he listened for any sound that might denote suspicion or alarm. There was none. Keys turned, doors clashed, footsteps passed along distant passages. No cry was raised, or hurry made, that seemed unusual.

Breathing more freely in a little while, he sat down

at the table and listened again, until the clock struck two. Sounds that he was not afraid of, for he divined their meaning, then began to be audible. Several doors were opened in succession, and finally his own.

A jailer, with a list in his hand, looked in, merely saying, "Follow me, Evremonde." And he followed into a large, dark room at a distance.

It was a dark, winter day, and what with the shadows within and what with the shadows without, he could but dimly discern the others who were brought there to have their arms bound. Some were standing, some were seated, some were lamenting and in restless motion, but these were few. The great majority were silent and still, looking fixedly at the ground.

As he stood by the wall in a dim corner, a young woman, with a slight, girlish form and a sweet, spare face, in which there was no vestige of color, and large widely-opened patient eyes, rose from the seat where he had observed her sitting and came to speak to him.

"Citizen Evremonde," she said, touching him with her

cold hands, "I am a poor little seamstress who was with you in La Force."

He murmured for answer, "True. I forget what you were accused of."

"Plots. Though the just Heaven knows I am innocent of any. Is it likely? Who would think of plotting with a poor, little, weak creature like me?" The forlorn smile with which she said it so touched him, that tears started from his eyes.

"If I may ride with you, Citizen Evremonde, will you let me hold your hand? I am not afraid, but I am little and weak, and it will give me more courage."

As the patient eyes were lifted to his face, he saw a sudden doubt in them, and then astonishment. He pressed the work-worn hunger-worn young fingers and touched his lips.

"Are you dying for him?" she whispered.

"And his wife and child. Shh. Yes."

"Oh, you will let me hold your brave hands, stranger?"

"Shh. Yes, my poor sister, to the last."

The same shadows that are falling on the prison are falling in that same hour of the early afternoon on the barrier, with the crowd about it, when a coach going out of Paris drives up to be examined.

"Who goes there? Whom have we within? Papers!"

The papers are handed out and read. "Alexander Manette, physician, French. Which is he?"

This is he. This helpless, inarticulately murmuring, wandering old man, pointed out.

"Apparently the citizen doctor is not in his right mind. The Revolution fever will have been too much for him."

Greatly, too much for him.

"Huh, many suffer with it. Lucie, his daughter, French. Which is she?"

This is she.

"Eh, apparently must be. Lucie the wife of Evremonde, is it not?"

It is.

"Huh, Evremonde, has an assignation as well? Eh?
Lucie, her child, English. This is she?"

She and no other.

"Sydney Carton, Advocate, English. Which is he?"

"He lies here, in this corner of the carriage," He
too is pointed out.

"Eh, apparently the English advocate is in a swoon."

It is hoped he will recover in the fresher air. It
is represented that he is not in strong health, and has
separated, sadly, from a friend who is under the
displeasure of the Republic.

"Ah, is that all? It is not a great deal, that!
Many are under the displeasure of the Republic, and must
look out at the little window, uh? Jarvis Lorry,
Banker, English. Which is he?"

"I am he, necessarily, being the last."

"I behold your papers, Jarvis Lorry, countersigned."

"One can depart, citizen?"

"One can depart. Forward, my postilions. A good
journey."

Along the Paris streets, the death carts rumble, hollow and harsh. Six tumbrels carry the day's wine to La Guillotine. All the devouring and insatiate monsters imagined, since imagination could record itself, are fused in the one realization, Guillotine.

There is a guard of sundry horsemen, riding abreast of the tumbrels, and faces are often turned up to some of them, and they are asked some question.

"Which is Evremonde?" says a man.

"That, in the back there."

"With his hand in the girl's?"

"Yes."

The man cries of, "Down Evremonde! To the guillotine all aristocrats! Down Evremonde!"

The supposed Evremonde descends, and the seamstress is lifted out next, after him. He has not relinquished her patient hand in getting out, but, still holds it as he promised. He gently places her with her back to the crashing engine that constantly whirs up and falls. And, she looks into his face and thanks him.

"But for you, dear stranger, I should not be so composed. For I am naturally a poor little thing, faint of heart. Nor should I have been able to raise my thoughts to Him, who was put to death, that we might have hope and comfort here today. I think you were sent to me by Heaven."

She kisses his lips. He kisses hers. They solemnly bless each other. The spare hand does not tremble as he releases it. Nothing worse than a sweet, bright constancy is in the patient face. She goes next before him--is gone!

"I am the resurrection and the life sayeth the Lord, he that believeth in me, though he were dead, yet, shall he live; and whosoever liveth and believeth in me, shall never die."

The murmuring of many voices, the upturning of many faces, the pressing on of many footsteps in the outskirts of the crowd, so that it swirls forward in a mass, like one great heave of water--all, flashes away.

They said of him about the city that night that it

was the peacefulest man's face ever beheld there. Many added that he looked sublime and prophetic.

One of the most remarkable sufferers by the same ax, a woman, had asked at the foot of the same scaffold, not long before, to be allowed to write down the thoughts that were inspiring her.

If he had given utterance to his, and they were prophetic, they would have been these:

'I see long ranks of the new oppressors who have risen on the destruction of the old, perishing by this retributive instrument, before it shall cease out of its present use. I see a beautiful city and a brilliant people, rising from this abyss and, in their struggles to be truly free, in their triumphs and defeats, through long years to come, I see the evil of this time, and of the previous time of which this is the natural birth, gradually making expiation for itself and wearing out. I see the lives for which I lay down my life, peaceful, useful, prosperous and happy, in that England which I shall see no more. I see that I hold a sanctuary in their hearts and in the hearts of their descendants, generations hence. I see her, an old woman, weeping for me on the anniversary of this day. I see her and her husband, their course done, lying side by side in their last earthly bed, and I know that each was not more honored and held sacred in the other's soul, than I was in the souls of both. It is a far, far better thing that I do, than I have ever done. It is a far, far better rest that I go to, than I have ever known.'

TITLE	AUTHOR	READER
Little Women	Louisa M. Alcott	Carol Drinkwater
Emma	Jane Austin	Dame Peggy Ashcroft
Pride and Prejudice	Jane Austin	Celia Johnson
Jane Eyre	Charlotte Bronte	Dame Wendy Hiller
Wuthering Heights	Emily Bronte	Daniel Massey
The Secret Garden	France Hodgson Burnett	Gwen Watford
Alice in Wonderland	Lewis Carroll	William Rushton
Through the Looking Glass	Lewis Carroll	William Rushton
Pinocchio	Carlo Collodi	Clive Dunn
The Manchurian Candidate	Richard Condon	Robert Vaughn
The Red Badge of Courage	Stephen Crane	Richard Crenna
A Christmas Carol	Charles Dickens	Leonard Rossiter
A Tale of Two Cities	Charles Dickens	John Carson
Great Expectations	Charles Dickens	Anton Rodgers
Oliver Twist	Charles Dickens	Ron Moody
A Study in Scarlet	Sir Arthur Conan Doyle	Tony Britton
The Hound of the Baskervilles	Sir Arthur Conan Doyle	Hugh Burden
The Lost World	Sir Arthur Conan Doyle	James Mason
The Sign of Four	Sir Arthur Conan Doyle	Tony Britton
Break In	Dick Francis	Nigel Havers
The Man of Property	John Galsworthy	Sir Michael Horden
The Wind in The Willows	Kenneth Grahame	Kenneth Williams
Grimm's Fairy Tales	The Brothers Grimm	Sheila Hancock
The Mayor of Casterbridge	Thomas Hardy	Alan Bates
The Hunchback of Notre Dame	Victor Hugo	Sir Anthony Quayle
The Prisoner of Zenda	Anthony Hope	Douglas Fairbanks Jr.
The Turn of the Screw	Henry James	Susannah York
The Jungle Book	Rudyard Kipling	Windsor Davies
Kim	Rudyard Kipling	Ben Cross
Call of the Wild	Jack London	Stewart Granger
Moby Dick	Herman Melville	George Kennedy
The Railway Children	E. Nesbit	Dinah Sheridan
Tales of Mystery and Horror	Edgar Allan Poe	Christopher Lee
Tales of Horror	Edgar Allan Poe	Christopher Lee
Guys and Dolls of Broadway	Damon Runyon	Jerry Orbach
Black Beauty	Anna Sewell	Hayley Mills
Heidi	Joanna Spyri	Petula Clark
Kidnapped	Robert Louis Stevenson	Bill Simpson
Treasure Island	Robert Louis Stevenson	Anthony Bate
The Adventures of Huckleberry Finn	Mark Twain	Dick Cavett
The Adventures of Tom Sawyer	Mark Twain	Robby Benson
The Time Machine	H.G. Wells	Robert Hardy
The Picture of Dorian Gray	Oscar Wilde	Peter Egan

TO ORDER BY PHONE
In Toronto **1-(416)-443-9322** Toll Free **1-(800)-387-8023**
Niagara Falls, N.Y. **1-(716)-298-5991** Toll Free **1-(800)-843-8056**
New York Residents Call Collect